W9-BRR-838

NEW YORK REVIEW BOOKS

CLASSICS

A HIGH WIND IN JAMAICA

RICHARD HUGHES (1900–1976) attended Oxford and lived for most of his life in a castle in Wales. His other books include *The Fox in the Attic* and *The Wooden Shepherdess*, the first two volumes of "The Human Predicament," an unfinished trilogy about the rise of German Fascism and the onset of World War II.

FRANCINE PROSE is the author of nine novels, two story collections, and most recently a collection of novellas, *Guided Tours of Hell*. Her stories and essays have appeared in numerous publications.

A HIGH WIND IN JAMAICA

Richard Hughes

■

Introduction by

FRANCINE PROSE

NEW YORK REVIEW BOOKS

New York

A HIGH WIND IN JAMAICA

Copyright © 1929 by the Executors of the Estate of Richard Hughes
Introduction Copyright © 1999 by Francine Prose
All rights reserved.

Reprinted by arrangement with the Estate of Richard Hughes
First published by Harper and Brothers 1929

This edition published in 1999 in the United States of America by
The New York Review of Books
1755 Broadway
New York, NY 10019

3 5 7 9 10 8 6 4 2

Library of Congress Cataloging-in-Publication Data

Hughes, Richard Arthur Warren, 1900–1976.
    [Innocent voyage]
    A high wind in Jamaica / Richard Hughes; introduction by
Francine Prose.
        p.   cm.
    Originally published: The innocent voyage. Boston: Harper, 1929.
    ISBN 0-940322-15-3 (pbk.: alk. paper)
    1. Children—Fiction. 2. Pirates—Fiction. I. Title.
PR6015.U35H5   1999
823'.912—dc 21   99-14565

ISBN 0-940322-15-3

Printed in the United States of America on acid-free paper.
September 1999
www.nybooks.com

INTRODUCTION

FIRST THE VAGUE premonitory chill—familiar, seduc-
tive, unwelcome—then the syrupy aura coating the visible world, through which its colors and edges appear ever
more lurid and sharp . . . The experience of reading Richard
Hughes's *A High Wind in Jamaica* (a book in which
swoons and febrile states play a critical role) evokes the
somatic sensations of falling ill, as a child. Indeed it recalls much about childhood that we thought (or might
have wished) we had forgotten, while it labors with sly
intelligence to dismantle the moral constructs that our
adult selves have so painstakingly assembled.

The book opens among the ruined houses of the West
Indies, slave quarters and mansions democratically lev-
eled by "earthquake, fire, rain, and deadlier vegetation,"

and features a frightening cameo appearance of the Misses Parkers, a pair of bedridden elderly heiresses starved to death by their servants amid ormolu clocks and the bloodied feathers of slaughtered chickens. The scene is grim, fantastical, but the novel's language is delicate and precise—there is a humorous, chirpy cerebration to its narrative voice—and right away we are conscious of, and troubled by, the dissonance between tone and content—one that turns out, however, to be central to the shocking story Hughes has to tell. For on the surface, *A High Wind in Jamaica* is an adventure yarn involving five British children captured by a crew of pirates. But underneath this high-spirited romp is a story about murder, senseless violence, gothic sexuality, and capricious betrayal, a narrative that more nearly evokes the pictures of the "outsider" artist Henry Darger than those of, say, Kate Greenaway.

When we first meet the Bas-Thornton family, they are living in Jamaica, where Mr. Thornton is involved in "business of some kind." The children have business of their own, most of it involving the serial cruelty with which they treat the island's hapless indigenous fauna. In this "paradise for English children," John, the eldest son, catches rats for the degustation and sport of Tabby, the family's half-wild pet cat, itself fond of mortal combat with poisonous snakes. Emily, the oldest of three girls, whose deeply peculiar experience and consciousness is at the center of the novel, has a passion for "catching house-lizards without their dropping their tails off, which they do when frightened. . . . Her room was full of these and other pets, some alive, others probably dead."

The younger Thorntons' sphere is so distant—so different—from that of their parents that they might as well be feral children. Mr. and Mrs. Thornton have no idea who their offspring are, or about the steamy, highly charged dramas that they are secretly enacting. "This sort of life was very peaceful, and might be excellent for nervy children like John; but a child like Emily, thought Mrs. Thornton, who is far from nervy, really needs some sort of stimulus and excitement, or there is a danger of her mind going to sleep altogether for ever. This life was too vegetable." It takes a typhoon blowing the roof off the family house—an event upstaged for the children by Tabby's murder by a pack of wild cats amidst thunder and lightning—before the grown-up Thorntons decide that the island life really is unsuitable, and send their brood off to Britain on the *Clorinda*.

By this point, Hughes has subjected us to a kind of Pavlovian conditioning: every time an animal appears, we brace ourselves for the worst. But even this protective recoil cannot quite prepare us for the grisly scene in which the crew of the *Clorinda* attempts to amputate a monkey's cancerous tail—and in the ensuing mayhem, are overtaken and captured by pirates. Nor can we possibly anticipate the brutality that transpires later, while the pirates are pleasantly occupied with their riotous efforts to make the circus lion and tiger fight. Throughout the book, both nature and human nature are sinister, threatening. The physicality of animal life—when Emily goes for a swim, "hundreds of infant fish were tickling with their inquisitive mouths every inch of her body, a sort of expressionless light kissing"—is "abominable." The setting sun—"unusually large and red, as if he threatened something peculiar"—seems predatory and perverted. The children themselves are, essentially, animate Petri dishes in which a "diabolic yeast" proliferates, and our initial fondness for the bumbling pirates is tempered by some nasty scenes. Captain Jonsen's drunken display of murky attention leads Emily to defend herself by biting his thumb, and later there is a creepy moment when he looks in on the sleeping children and, knowing that Emily is awake and watching, flicks his fingernail against baby Laura's bare and upraised bottom.

Hughes is not afraid to dwell on startling, uncomfortable verities about the world and its inhabitants, and one of the things he does most impressively in *A High Wind in Jamaica* is to put a wicked spin on the Romantic notion of the child—the Wordsworthian innocent-savant. He suggests that children are closer than adults to nature, that the way that they view sex—mysterious, fascinating, incomprehensible, repulsive, responsible for weird alliances and even stranger behavior—is the way sex really is. Passion between consenting adults is a polite convention compared to the immediate realities of the flashy, "twittering" drag queens who assist the pirates in the capture of the *Clorinda*, or the night Emily gets to spend in bed with a pet alligator, or the suffocating kisses little Edward receives from a fat, mustachioed old woman who grabs him during the pirates' Cuban layover ("Edward could no more have struggled than if caught by a boa. Moreover, the portentous woman fascinated him, as if she had been a boa indeed. He lay in her arms limp, self-conscious, and dejected: but without active thought of escape.")

The confusions and seductions, horrors and comforts of Emily's relationship with the captain, and later with the bewitching Louisa Dawson—a passenger on the steamer to which the pirates eventually surrender the children, and which brings them to England—belong to the same polymorphous realm of attraction and repugnance as her encounter with the kissing fish. The captain amuses himself by drawing the sort of sexual doodles that might be done by a young boy. At one point he draws over the figures Emily has penciled on the wall of her bunk:

> Jonsen could only draw two things: ships, and naked
> women. . . . He took the pencil: and before long there
> began to appear between Emily's crude uncertain
> lines round thighs, rounder bellies, high swelling
> bosoms, all somewhat in the manner of Rubens.

This scene of a grown man amending a girl's scribblings has an upsetting, sensational edge that recalls a child's skewed perspective on physicality; it is all the more disturbing for its weird aspect of innocence.

If adult sexuality seems unhealthily like a child's, adult morality is hardly more mature or developed. Everyone lies and keeps poisonous secrets, especially the children. ("Grown-ups embark on a life of deception with considerable misgivings, and generally fail. But not so children. A child can hide the most appalling secret without the least effort, and is practically secure against detection.") Everyone, of every age, behaves according to an almost psychotically private and individual set of moral criteria: it's wrong to mention underwear and call adults by their first names but permissible (or hardly worth noting) to lie to God in one's prayers and misdirect a court of law convened to try a capital offense. No one has much of a memory; the children adapt quickly to separation from their parents and recover from the shock of a death among them with alarming ease and flexibility.

By the end of the book, what the children have been told about their ordeal by the adults (who themselves have little or no interest in the truth) has blended with, or replaced, their sense of what really occurred. And when we meet the lawyers directing the trial that occupies the final section of the novel, we realize that these representatives of justice and high civilization—after all that wildness!—are little better than pirates in robes and periwigs. They are men, Hughes slyly informs us, whose interest in the world is the opposite of a writer's: "It is the novelist who is concerned with facts, whose job it is to say what a particular man did do on a particular occasion: the lawyer does not, cannot be expected to go further than to show what the ordinary man would be most likely to do under presumed circumstances."

Unlike William Golding's far more simplistic *The Lord of the Flies*, to which it is sometimes compared, Richard Hughes's novel resists any attempts to extract from it a moral or sociological lesson, a bit of received wisdom or home truth. It's hard, in fact, to think of another fiction so blithe in its refusal to throw us the tiniest crumb of solace or consolation, to present a single character who functions as a lodestar of rectitude or beneficence.

In the end, everything in this luminous, extraordinary novel is so much the reverse of what we think it should be, or what we would expect, that we are left entirely disoriented—unsure of what anything is, or should be. The effect is disturbing and yet beautiful, fantastic but also frighteningly true to life. Published in 1929, just as history was preparing events that would forever revise the terms in which one could talk about innocence and evil, *A High Wind in Jamaica* is one of those prescient works of art that seems somehow to have caught (on the breeze, as it were) a warning scent of danger and blood—that is to say, of the future.

—FRANCINE PROSE

A
HIGH WIND
IN
JAMAICA

1

ONE OF THE fruits of Emancipation in the West Indian islands is the number of the ruins, either attached to the houses that remain or within a stone's throw of them: ruined slaves' quarters, ruined sugar-grinding houses, ruined boiling houses; often ruined mansions that were too expensive to maintain. Earthquake, fire, rain, and deadlier vegetation, did their work quickly.

One scene is very clear in my mind, in Jamaica. There was a vast stone-built house called Derby Hill (where the Parkers lived). It had been the center of a very prosperous plantation. With Emancipation, like many others, that went *bung*. The sugar buildings fell down. Bush smothered the cane and guinea-grass. The field negroes left their cottages in a body, to be somewhere less disturbed by even the possibility of work. Then the house negroes' quarters burned down, and the three remaining faithful servants occupied the mansion. The two heiresses of all this, the Miss Parkers, grew old; and were by education incapable. And the scene is this: coming to Derby Hill on some business or other, and wading waist-deep in bushes up to the front door, now lashed permanently open by a rank plant. The jalousies of the house had been all torn down, and then supplanted as darkeners, by powerful vines: and out of this crumbling half-vegetable gloom an old negress peered, wrapped in filthy brocade. The two old Miss Parkers lived in bed, for the negroes had taken away all their clothes: they were nearly starved. Drinking water was brought, in two cracked Worcester cups and three coconut shells on a silver salver. Presently one of the heiresses persuaded her tyrants to lend her an old print dress, and came and pottered about in the mess half-heartedly: tried to wipe the old blood and feathers of slaughtered chickens from a gilt and marble table: tried to talk sensibly: tried to wind an ormolu clock: and then gave it up and mooned away back to bed. Not long after this, I believe, they were both starved altogether to death. Or, if that were hardly possible in so prolific a country, perhaps given ground glass—rumor varied. At any rate, they died.

That is the sort of scene which makes a deep impression on the mind; far deeper than the ordinary, less romantic, everyday thing which shows the real state of an island in the statistical sense. Of course, even in the transition period one only found melodrama like this in rare patches. More truly typical was Ferndale, for instance, an estate about fifteen miles away from Derby Hill. Only the overseer's house here remained: the Big House had altogether collapsed and been smothered over. It consisted of a ground floor of stone, given over to goats and the children, and a first floor of wood, the inhabited part, reached from outside by a double flight of wooden steps. When the earthquakes came the upper part only slid about a little, and could be jacked back into position with big levers. The roof was of shingles: after very dry weather it leaked like a sieve, and the first few days of the rainy season would be spent in a perpetual general-post of beds and other furniture to escape the drips, until the wood swelled.

The people who lived there at the time I have in mind were the Bas-Thorntons: not natives of the Island, "Creoles," but a family from England. Mr. Bas-Thornton had a business of some kind in St. Anne's, and used to ride there every day on a mule. He had such long legs that his stunted mount made him look rather ridiculous: and being quite as temperamental as a mule himself, a quarrel between the two was generally worth watching.

Close to the dwelling were the ruined grinding and boiling houses. These two are never quite cheek by jowl:

the grinding house is set on higher ground, with a water-wheel to turn the immense iron vertical rollers. From these the cane juice runs down a wedge-shaped trough to the boiling house, where a negro stands and rinses a little lime-wash into it with a grass brush to make it granulate. Then it is emptied into big copper vats, over furnaces burning faggots and "trash," or squeezed-out cane. There a few negroes stand, skimming the poppling vats with long-handled copper ladles, while their friends sit round, eating sugar or chewing trash, in a mist of hot vapor. What they skim off oozes across the floor with an admixture of a good deal of filth—insects, even rats, and whatever sticks to negroes' feet—into another basin, thence to be distilled into rum.

This, at any rate, is how it used to be done. I know nothing of modern methods—or if there are any, never having visited the island since 1860, which is a long time ago now.

But long before that year all this was over at Ferndale: the big copper vats were overturned, and up in the grinding-house the three great rollers lay about loose. No water reached it: the stream had gone about its own business elsewhere. The Bas-Thornton children used to crawl into the cut-well through the vent, among dead leaves and the wreck of the wheel. There, one day, they found a wild-cat's nest, with the mother away. The kittens were tiny, and Emily tried to carry them home in her pinafore; but they bit and scratched so fiercely, right through her thin frock, that she was very glad—except for pride—that they all escaped but one. This one, Tom, grew up: though he was never really tamed. Later he begat several litters on an old tame cat they had, Kitty Cranbrook; and the only survivor of this progeny, Tabby, became rather a famous cat in his way. (But Tom soon took to the jungle altogether.) Tabby was faithful, and a good swimmer, which he would do for pleasure, sculling around the bathing-pool behind the children, giving an occasional yowl of excitement. Also, he had mortal sport with snakes: would wait for a rattler or a black-snake like a mere mouse: drop on it from a tree or somewhere, and fight it to death. Once he got bitten, and they all wept bitterly, expecting to see a spectacular death-agony; but he just went off into the bush and probably ate something, for he came back in a few days quite cock-a-hoop and as ready to eat snakes as ever.

Red-headed John's room was full of rats: he used to catch them in big gins, and then let them go for Tabby to dispatch. Once the cat was so impatient he seized trap and all and caterwauled off into the night banging it on the stones and sending up showers of sparks. Again he returned in a few days, very sleek and pleased: but John never saw his trap again. Another plague of his were the bats, which also infested his room in hundreds.

Mr. Bas-Thornton could crack a stockwhip, and used to kill a bat on the wing with it most neatly. But the din this made in that little box of a room at midnight was infernal: earsplitting cracks, and the air already full of the tiny penetrating squeaks of the vermin.

It was a kind of paradise for English children to come to, whatever it might be for their parents: especially at that time, when no one lived in at all a wild way at home. Here one had to be a little ahead of the times: or decadent, whichever you like to call it. The difference between boys and girls, for instance, had to be left to look after itself. Long hair would have made the evening search for grass-ticks and nits interminable: Emily and Rachel had their hair cut short, and were allowed to do everything the boys did—to climb trees, swim, and trap animals and birds: they even had two pockets in their frocks.

It was round the bathing-pool their life centered, more than the house. Every year, when the rains were over, a dam was built across the stream, so that all through the dry season there was quite a large pool to swim in. There were trees all round: enormous fluffed cotton trees, with coffee trees between their paws, and log-wood, and gorgeous red and green peppers: amongst them, the pool was almost completely shaded. Emily and John set tree-springes in them—Lame-foot Sam taught them how. Cut a bendy stick, and tie a string to one end. Then sharpen the other, so that it can impale a fruit as bait. Just at the base of this point flatten it a little, and bore a hole through the flat part. Cut a little peg that will just stick in the mouth of this hole. Then make a loop in the end of the string: bend the stick, as in stringing a bow, till the loop will thread through the little hole, and jam it with the peg, along which the loop should lie spread. Bait the point, and hang it in a tree among the twigs: the bird alights on the peg to peck the fruit, the peg falls out, the loop whips tight round its ankles: then away up out of the water like pink predatory monkeys, and decide by "Eena, deena, dina, do," or some such rigmarole, whether to twist its neck or let it go free—thus the excitement and suspense, both for child and bird, can be prolonged beyond the moment of capture.

It was only natural that Emily should have great ideas of improving the negroes. They were, of course, Christians, so there was nothing to be done about their morals: nor were they in need of soup, or knitted things; but they were sadly ignorant. After a good deal of negotiation they consented in the end to let her teach Little Jim to read: but she had no success. Also she had a passion for catching house-lizards without their dropping their tails off, which they do when frightened: it needed endless patience to get them whole and unalarmed into a matchbox. Catching green grass-lizards was also very delicate.

She would sit and whistle, like Orpheus, till they came out of their crannies and showed their emotion by puffing out their pink throats: then, very gently, she would lasso them with a long blade of grass. Her room was full of these and other pets, some alive, others probably dead. She also had tame fairies; and a familiar, or oracle, the White Mouse with an Elastic Tail, who was always ready to settle any point in question, and whose rule was a rule of iron—especially over Rachel, Edward, and Laura, the little ones (or Liddlies, as they came to be known in the family). To Emily, his interpreter, he allowed, of course, certain privileges: and with John, who was older than Emily, he quite wisely did not interfere.

He was omnipresent: the fairies were more localized, living in a small hole in the hill guarded by two dagger-plants.

The best fun at the bathing-pool was had with a big forked log. John would sit astride the main stem, and the others pushed him about by two prongs. The little ones, of course, only splashed about the shallow end: but John and Emily dived. John, that is to say, dived properly, head-foremost: Emily only jumped in feet first, stiff as a rod; but she, on the other hand, would go off higher boughs than he would. Once, when she was eight, Mrs. Thornton had thought she was too big to bathe naked any more. The only bathing-dress she could rig was an old cotton night-gown. Emily jumped in as usual: first the balloons of air tipped her upside down, and then the wet cotton wrapped itself round her head and arms and nearly drowned her. After that, decency was let go hang again: it is hardly worth being drowned for—at least, it does not at first sight appear to be.

But once a negro really was drowned in the pool. He had gorged himself full of stolen mangoes: and feeling guilty, thought he might as well also cool himself in the forbidden pond, and make one repentance cover two crimes. He could not swim, and had only a child (Little Jim) with him. The cold water and the surfeit brought on an apoplexy: Jim poked at him with a piece of stick a little, and then ran away in a fright. Whether the man died of the apoplexy or the drowning was a point for an inquest; and the doctor, after staying at Ferndale for a week, decided it was from drowning, but that he was full of green mangoes right up to his mouth. The great advantage of this was that no negro would bathe there again, for fear the dead man's "duppy," or ghost, should catch him. So if any black even came near while they were bathing, John and Emily would pretend the duppy had grabbed at them, and off he would go, terribly upset. Only one of the negroes at Ferndale had ever actually seen a duppy: but that was quite enough. They cannot be mistaken for living people, because their heads are turned backwards on their shoulders, and they carry a chain: moreover one must never call them duppies to their faces, as it gives them power. This poor man forgot, and called out "*Duppy!*" when he saw it. He got terrible rheumatics.

Lame-foot Sam told most stories. He used to sit all day on the stone barbecues where the pimento was dried, digging maggots out of his toes. This seemed at first very horrid to the children, but he seemed quite contented: and when jiggers got under their own skins, and laid their little bags of eggs there, it was not absolutely unpleasant. John used to get quite a sort of thrill from rubbing the place. Sam told them the Anansi stories: Anansi and the Tiger, and how Anansi looked after the Crocodile's nursery, and so on. Also he had a little poem which impressed them very much:

> Quacko Sam
> Him bery fine man:
> Him dance all de dances dat de darkies can:
> Him dance de schottische, him dance de Cod Reel:
> Him dance ebery kind of dance till him foot-
> bottom peel.

Perhaps that was how old Sam's own affliction first came about: he was very sociable. He was said to have a great many children.

II

The stream which fed the bathing-hole ran into it down a gully through the bush which offered an enticing vista for exploring: but somehow the children did not often go up it very far. Every stone had to be overturned in the hope of finding crayfish: or if not, John had to take a sporting gun, which he bulleted with spoonfuls of water to shoot humming-birds on the wing, too tiny frail quarry for any solider projectile. For, only a few yards up, there was a Frangipani tree: a mass of brilliant blossom and no leaves, which was almost hidden in a cloud of humming-birds so vivid as much to outshine the flowers. Writers have often lost their way trying to explain how brilliant a jewel the humming-bird is: it cannot be done.

They build their wee woollen nests on the tops of twigs, where no snake can reach them. They are devoted to their eggs, and will not move though you touch them. But they are so delicate the children never did that: they held their breath and stared and stared—and were out-stared.

Somehow the celestial vividness of this barrier generally arrested them: it was seldom they explored further: only once, I think, on a day when Emily was feeling peculiarly irritated.

It was her own tenth birthday. They had frittered away all the morning in the glass-like gloom of the bathing-hole. Now John sat naked on the bank making a wicker trap. In the shallows the small ones rolled and chuckled. Emily, for coolness, sat up to her chin in water, and hundreds of infant fish were tickling with their inquisitive mouths every inch of her body, a sort of expressionless light kissing.

Anyhow she had lately come to hate being touched— but this was abominable. At last, when she could stand it no longer, she clambered out and dressed. Rachel and Laura were too small for a long walk: and the last thing, she felt, that she wanted was to have one of the boys with her: so she stole quietly past John's back, scowling balefully at him for no particular reason. Soon she was out of sight among the bushes.

She pushed on rather fast, not taking much notice of things, up the river bed for about three miles. She had never been so far afield before. Then her attention was caught by a clearing leading down to the water: and here was the source of the river. She caught her breath delightedly: it bubbled up clear and cold, through three distinct springs, under a clump of bamboos, just as a river should: the greatest possible find, and a private discovery of her own. She gave instantaneous inward thanks to God for thinking of such a perfect birthday treat, especially as things had seemed to be going all wrong: and then began to ferret in the limestone sources with the whole length of her arm, among the ferns and cresses.

Hearing a splash, she looked round. Some half-dozen strange negro children had come down the clearing to fetch water and were staring at her in astonishment. Emily stared back. In sudden terror they flung down their calabashes and galloped away up the clearing like hares. Immediately, but with dignity, Emily followed them. The clearing narrowed to a path, and the path led in a very short time to a village.

It was all ragged and unkempt, and shrill with voices. There were small one-storey wattle huts dotted about, completely overhung by the most enormous trees. There was no sort of order: they appeared anywhere: there were no railings, and only one or two of the most terribly starved, mangy cattle to keep in or out. In the middle of all was an indeterminate quagmire or muddy pond, where a group of half-naked negroes, and totally naked black children, and a few brown ones, were splashing with geese and ducks.

Emily stared: they stared back. She made a movement towards them: they separated at once into the various huts, and watched her from there. Encouraged by the comfortable feeling of inspiring fright she advanced, and at last found an old creature who would talk: Dis Liberty Hill, dis Black Man's Town, Old-time niggers, dey go fer run from de bushas (overseers), go fer live here. De piccaninnies, dey never see buckras (whites) . . . And so on. It was a refuge, built by runaway slaves, and still inhabited.

And then, that her cup of happiness might be full, some of the bolder children crept out and respectfully offered her flowers—really to get a better look at her pallid face. Her heart bubbled up in her, she swelled with glory: and taking leave with the greatest condescension she trod all the long way home on veritable air, back to her beloved family, back to a birthday cake wreathed with stephanotis, lit with ten candles, and in which it so happened that the sixpenny piece was invariably found in the birthday-person's slice.

III

This was, fairly typically, the life of an English family in Jamaica. Mostly these only stayed a few years. The Creoles—families who had been in the West Indies for more than one generation—gradually evolved something a little more distinctive. They lost some of the traditional mental mechanism of Europe, and the outlines of a new one began to appear.

There was one such family the Bas-Thorntons were acquainted with, who had a ramshackle estate to the eastward. They invited John and Emily to spend a couple of days with them, but Mrs. Thornton was in two minds about letting them go, lest they should learn bad ways. The children there were a wildish lot, and, in the morning at least, would often run about barefoot like negroes, which is a very important point in a place like Jamaica where the whites have to keep up appearances. They had a governess whose blood was possibly not pure, and who used to beat the children ferociously with a hair-brush. However, the climate at the Fernandez's place was healthy, and also Mrs. Thornton thought it good for them to have some intercourse with other children outside their own family, however undesirable: and she let them go.

It was the afternoon after that birthday, and a long buggy-ride. Both fat John and thin Emily were speechless and solemn with excitement: it was the first visit they had ever paid. Hour after hour the buggy labored over the uneven road. At last the lane to Exeter, the Fernandez's place, was reached. It was evening, the sun about to do his rapid tropical setting. He was unusually large and red, as if he threatened something peculiar. The lane, or drive, was gorgeous: for the first few hundred yards it was entirely hedged with "seaside grapes," clusters of fruit half-way between a gooseberry and a golden pippin, with here and there the red berries of coffee trees newly planted among the burnt stumps in a clearing, but already neglected. Then a massive stone gateway in a sort of Colonial-Gothic style. This had to be circumvented: no one had taken the trouble to heave open the heavy gates for years. There was no fence, nor ever had been, so the track simply passed it by.

And beyond the gates an avenue of magnificent cabbage-palms. No tree, not oldest beech nor chestnut, is more spectacular in an avenue: rising a sheer hundred feet with no break in the line before the actual crown of plumes; and palm upon palm, palm upon palm, like a heavenly double row of pillars, leading on interminably, till even the huge house was dwarfed into a sort of ultimate mouse-trap.

As they journeyed on between these palms the sun went suddenly down, darkness flooded up round them out of the ground, retorted to almost immediately by the moon. Presently, shimmering like a ghost, an old blind white donkey stood in their way. Curses did not move him: the driver had to climb down and push him aside. The air was full of the usual tropic din: mosquitoes humming, cicalas trilling, bull-frogs twanging like guitars. That din goes on all night and all day almost: is more insistent, more memorable than the heat itself, even, or the number of things that bite. In the valley beneath the fireflies came to life: as if at a signal passed along, wave after wave after wave of light swept down the gorge. From a neighboring hill the cockatoos began their serenade, an orchestration of drunk men laughing against iron girders tossed at each other and sawn up with rusty hack-saws: the most awful noise. But Emily and John, so far as they noticed it at all, found it vaguely exhilarating. Through it could presently be distinguished another sound: a negro praying. They soon came near him: where an orange tree loaded with golden fruit gleamed dark and bright in the moonlight, veiled in the pinpoint scintillation of a thousand fire-flies sat the old black saint among the branches, talking loudly, drunkenly, and confidentially with God.

Almost unexpectedly they came on the house, and were whisked straight off to bed. Emily omitted to wash, since there seemed such a hurry, but made up for it by spending an unusually long time over her prayers. She pressed her eyeballs devoutly with her fingers to make sparks appear, in spite of the slightly sick feeling it always induced: and then, already sound asleep, clambered, I suppose, into bed.

The next day the sun rose as he had set: large, round, and red. It was blindingly hot, foreboding. Emily, who woke early in a strange bed, stood at the window watching the negroes release the hens from the chicken-houses, where they were shut up at night for fear of John-crows. As each bird hopped sleepily out, the black passed his hand over its stomach to see if it meditated an egg that day: if so, it was confined again, or it would have gone off and laid in the bush. It was already as hot as an oven.

Another black, with eschatological yells and tail-twistings and lassoings, was confining a cow in a kind of pillory, that it might have no opportunity of sitting down while being milked. The poor brute's hooves were aching with the heat, its miserable tea-cup of milk fevered in its ud-der. Even as she stood at the shady window Emily felt as sweaty as if she had been running. The ground was fis-sured with drought.

Margaret Fernandez, whose room Emily was sharing, slipped out of bed silently and stood beside her, wrinkling the short nose in her pallid face.

"Good morning," said Emily politely.

"Smells like an earthquake," said Margaret, and dressed. Emily remembered the awful story about the governess and the hair-brush: certainly Margaret did not use one for its ordinary purpose, though she had long hair: so it must be true.

Margaret was ready long before Emily, and banged out of the room. Emily followed later, neat and nervous, to find no one. The house was empty. Presently she spied John under a tree, talking to a negro boy. By his off-hand manner Emily guessed he was telling *disproportionate* stories (not *lies*) about the importance of Ferndale com-pared with Exeter. She did not call him, because the house was silent and it was not her place, as guest, to al-ter anything: so she went out to him. Together they circumnavigated: they found a stable-yard, and negroes preparing ponies, and the Fernandez children, barefoot even as Rumor had whispered. Emily caught her breath, shocked. Even at that moment a chicken, scuttling across the yard, trod on a scorpion and tumbled over stark dead as if shot. But it was not so much the danger which upset Emily as the unconventionality.

"Come on," said Margaret: "it's much too hot to stay about here. We'll go down to Exeter Rocks."

The cavalcade mounted—Emily very conscious of her boots, buttoned respectably half-way up her calf. Somebody had food, and calabashes of water. The ponies evidently knew the way. The sun was still red and large: the sky above cloudless, and like blue glaze poured over baking clay: but close over the ground a dirty gray haze hovered. As they followed the lane towards the sea they came to a place where, yesterday, a fair-sized spring had bubbled up by the roadside. Now it was dry. But even as they passed a kind of gout of water gushed forth: and then it was dry again, although gurgling inwardly to itself. But the cavalcade were hot, far too hot to speak to one another: they sat their ponies as loosely as possible, longing for the sea.

The morning advanced. The heated air grew quite easily hotter, as if from some reserve of enormous blaze on which it could draw at will. Bullocks only shifted their stinging feet when they could bear the soil no longer:

even the insects were too languorous to pipe, the basking lizards hid themselves and panted. It was so still you could have heard the least buzz a mile off. Not a naked fish would willingly move his tail. The ponies advanced because they must. The children ceased even to muse.

They all very nearly jumped out of their skins; for close at hand a crane had trumpeted once desperately. Then the broken silence closed down as flawless as before. They perspired twice as violently with the stimulus. Their pace grew slower and slower. It was no faster than a procession of snails that at last they reached the sea.

Exeter Rocks is a famous place. A bay of the sea, almost a perfect semicircle, guarded by the reef: shelving white sands to span the few feet from the water to the under-cut turf: and then, almost at the mid point, a jutting-out shelf of rocks right into deep water—fathoms deep. And a narrow fissure in the rocks, leading the water into a small pool, or miniature lagoon, right inside their bastion. There it was, safe from sharks or drowning, that the Fernandez children meant to soak themselves all day, like turtles in a crawl. The water of the bay was as smooth and immovable as basalt, yet clear as the finest gin: albeit the swell muttered a mile away on the reef. The water within the pool itself could not reasonably be smoother. No sea-breeze thought of stirring. No bird trespassed on the inert air.

For a while they had not energy to get into the water, but lay on their faces, looking down, down, down, at the sea-fans and sea-feathers, the scarlet-plumed barnacles and corals, the black and yellow schoolmistress-fish, the rainbow-fish—all that forest of ideal christmas trees which is a tropical sea-bottom. Then they stood up, giddy and seeing black, and in a trice were floating suspended in water like drowned ones, only their noses above the surface, under the shadow of a rocky ledge.

An hour or so after noon they clustered together, puffy from the warm water, in the insufficient shade of a Panama fern: ate such of the food they had brought as they had appetite for; and drank all the water, wishing for more. Then a very odd thing happened: for even as they sat there they heard the most peculiar sound: a strange, rushing sound that passed overhead like a gale of wind—but not a breath of breeze stirred, that was the odd thing: followed by a sharp hissing and hurtling, like a flight of rockets, or gigantic swans—very distant rocs, perhaps—on the wing. They all looked up: but there was nothing at all. The sky was empty and lucid. Long before they were back in the water again all was still. Except that after a while John noticed a sort of tapping, as if some one were gently knocking the outside of a bath you were in. But the bath they were in had no outside, it was solid world. It was funny.

By sunset they were so weak from long immersion they could barely stand up, and as salted as bacon: but, with some common impulse, just before the sun went down they all left the rocks and went and stood by their clothes, where the ponies were tethered, under some palms. As he sank the sun grew even larger: and instead of red was now a sodden purple. Down he went, behind the western horn of the bay, which blackened till its water-line disappeared and substance and reflection seemed one sharp symmetrical pattern.

Not a breath of breeze even yet ruffled the water: yet momentarily it trembled of its own accord, shattering the reflections: then was glassy again. On that the children held their breath, waiting for it to happen.

A school of fish, terrified by some purely submarine event, thrust their heads right out of the water, squattering across the bay in an arrowy rush, dashing up sparkling ripples with the tiny heave of their shoulders: yet after each disturbance all was soon like hardest, dark, thick, glass.

Once things vibrated slightly, like a chair in a concert-room: and again there was that mysterious winging, though there was nothing visible beneath the swollen iridescent stars.

Then it came. The water of the bay began to ebb away, as if some one had pulled up the plug: a foot or so of sand and coral gleamed for a moment new to the air: then back the sea rushed in miniature rollers which splashed right up to the feet of the palms. Mouthfuls of turf were torn away: and on the far side of the bay a small piece of cliff tumbled into the water: sand and twigs showered down, dew fell from the trees like diamonds: birds and beasts, their tongues at last loosed, screamed and bellowed: the ponies, though quite unalarmed, lifted up their heads and yelled.

That was all: a few moments. Then silence, with a rapid countermarch, recovered all his rebellious kingdom. Stillness again. The trees moved as little as the pillars of a ruin, each leaf laid sleekly in place. The bubbling foam subsided: the reflections of the stars came out among it as if from clouds. Silent, still, dark, placid, as if there could never have been a disturbance. The naked children too continued to stand motionless beside the quiet ponies, dew on their hair and eyelashes, shine on their infantile round paunches.

But as for Emily, it was too much. The earthquake went completely to her head. She began to dance, hopping laboriously from one foot on to another. John caught the infection. He turned head over heels on the damp sand, over and over in an elliptical course, till before he knew it he was in the water, and so giddy as hardly to be able to tell up from down.

At that, Emily knew what it was she wanted to do. She scrambled on to a pony and galloped him up and down the beach, trying to bark like a dog. The Fernandez children stared, solemn but not disapproving. John, shaping a course for Cuba, was swimming as if sharks were paring his toe-nails. Emily rode her pony into the sea, and beat and beat him till he swam: and so she followed John towards the reef, yapping herself hoarse.

It must have been fully a hundred yards before they were spent. Then they turned for the shore, John holding on to Emily's leg, puffing and gasping, both a little over-done, their emotion run down. Presently John gasped:

"You shouldn't ride on your bare skin, you'll catch ringworm."

"I don't care if I do," said Emily.

"You would if you did," said John.

"I don't care!" chanted Emily.

It seemed a long way to the shore. When they reached it the others had dressed and were preparing to start. Soon the whole party were on their way home in the dark. Presently Margaret said:

"So that's that."

No one answered.

"I could smell it was an earthquake coming when I got up. Didn't I say so, Emily?"

"You and your smells!" said Jimmie Fernandez. "You're always smelling things!"

"She's awfully good at smells," said the youngest,

Harry, proudly, to John. "She can sort out people's dirty clothes for the wash by smell: who they belong to."

"She can't really," said Jimmie: "she fakes it. As if every one smelt different!"

"I can!"

"Dogs can, anyway," said John.

Emily said nothing. Of course people smelt different: it didn't need arguing. She could always tell her own towel from John's, for instance: or even knew if one of the others had used it. But it just showed what sort of people Creoles were, to *talk* about Smell, in that open way.

"Well, anyhow I said there was going to be an earthquake and there was one," said Margaret.

That was what Emily was waiting for! So it really had been an Earthquake (she had not liked to ask, it seemed so ignorant, but now Margaret had said in so many words that it was one).

If ever she went back to England, she could now say to people, "*I have been in an Earthquake.*"

With that certainty, her soused excitement began to revive. For there was nothing, no adventure from the hands of God or Man, to equal it. Realize that if she had suddenly found she could fly it would not have seemed more miraculous to her. Heaven had played its last, most terrible card; and small Emily had survived, where even grown men (such as Korah, Dathan, and Abiram) had succumbed.

Life seemed suddenly a little empty: for never again could there happen to her anything so dangerous, so sublime.

Meanwhile, Margaret and Jimmie were still arguing:

"Well, there's one thing, there'll be plenty of eggs to-morrow," said Jimmie. "There's nothing like an earthquake for making them lay."

How funny Creoles were! They didn't seem to realize the difference it made to a person's whole after-life to have been in an Earthquake.

When they got home, Martha, the black housemaid, had hard things to say about the sublime cataclysm. She had dusted the drawing-room china only the day before: and now everything was covered again in a fine penetrating film of dust.

IV

The next morning, Sunday, they went home. Emily was still so saturated in earthquake as to be dumb. She ate earthquake and slept earthquake: her fingers and legs were earthquake. With John it was ponies. The earthquake had been fun: but it was the ponies that mattered. But at present it did not worry Emily that she was alone in her sense of proportion. She was too completely possessed to be able to see anything, or realize that any one else pretended to even a self-delusive fiction of existence.

Their mother met them at the door. She bubbled questions: John chattered ponies, but Emily was still tongue-tied. She was, in her mind, like a child who has eaten too much even to be able to be sick.

Mrs. Thornton got a little worried about her at times. This sort of life was very peaceful, and might be excellent for nervy children like John: but a child like Emily, thought Mrs. Thornton, who is far from nervy, really needs some sort of stimulus and excitement, or there is a danger of her mind going to sleep altogether for ever. This life was too vegetable. Consequently Mrs. Thornton always spoke to Emily in her brightest manner, as if everything was of the greatest possible interest. She had hoped, too, the visit to Exeter might liven her up: but she had come back as silent and expressionless as ever. It had evidently made no impression on her at all.

John marshaled the small ones in the cellar, and round and round they marched, wooden swords at the slope, singing "Onward, Christian Soldiers." Emily did not join them. What did it now matter, that earlier woe, that being a girl she could never when grown up become a real soldier with a real sword? She had been in an Earthquake.

Nor did the others keep it up very long. (Sometimes they would go on for three or four hours.) For, whatever it might have done for Emily's soul, the earthquake had done little to clear the air. It was as hot as ever. In the animal world there seemed some strange commotion, as if they had wind of something. The usual lizards and mosquitoes were still absent: but in their place the earth's most horrid progeny, creatures of darkness, sought the open: land-crabs wandered about aimlessly, angrily twiddling their claws: and the ground seemed almost alive with red ants and cockroaches. Up on the roof the pigeons were gathered, talking to each other fearfully.

The cellar (or rather, ground floor), where they were playing, had no communication with the wooden structure above, but had an opening of its own under the twin flight of steps leading to the front door; and there the children presently gathered in the shadow. Out in the compound lay one of Mr. Thornton's best handkerchiefs. He must have dropped it that morning. But none of them felt the energy to go and retrieve it, out into the sun. Then, as they stood there, they saw Lame-foot Sam come limping across the yard. Seeing the prize, he was about to carry it off. Suddenly he remembered it was Sunday. He dropped it like a hot brick, and began to cover it with sand, exactly where he had found it.

"Please God, I thieve you to-morrow," he explained hopefully. "Please God, you still there?"

A low mutter of thunder seemed to offer grudging assent.

"Thank you, Lord," said Sam, bowing to a low bank of cloud. He hobbled off: but then, not too sure perhaps that Heaven would keep Its promise, changed his mind: snatched up the handkerchief and made off for his cottage. The thunder muttered louder and more angrily: but Sam ignored the warning.

It was the custom that, whenever Mr. Thornton had been to St. Anne's, John and Emily should run out to meet him, and ride back with him, one perched on each of his stirrups.

That Sunday evening they ran out as soon as they saw him coming, in spite of the thunderstorm that by now was clattering over their very heads—and not only over their heads either, for in the Tropics a thunderstorm is not a remote affair up in the sky, as it is in England, but is all round you: lightning plays ducks and drakes across the water, bounds from tree to tree, bounces about the ground, while the thunder seems to proceed from violent explosions in your own very core.

"Go back! Go back, you damned little fools!" he yelled furiously: "Get into the house!"

They stopped, aghast: and began to realize that after all it was a storm of more than ordinary violence. They discovered that they were drenched to the skin—must have been the moment they left the house. The lightning kept up a continuous blaze: it was playing about their father's very stirrup-irons; and all of a sudden they realized that he was afraid. They fled to the house, shocked to the heart: and he was in the house almost as soon as they were. Mrs. Thornton rushed out:

"My dear, I'm so glad . . ."

"I've never seen such a storm! Why on earth did you let the children come out?"

"I never dreamt they would be so silly! And all the time I was thinking—but thank Heaven you're back!"

"I think the worst is over now."

Perhaps it was; but all through supper the lightning shone almost without flickering. And John and Emily could hardly eat: the memory of that momentary look on their father's face haunted them.

It was an unpleasant meal altogether. Mrs. Thornton had prepared for her husband his "favorite dish": than which no action could more annoy a man of whim. In the middle of it all in burst Sam, ceremony dropped: he flung the handkerchief angrily on the table and stumped out.

"What on earth . . ." began Mr. Thornton.

But John and Emily knew: and thoroughly agreed with Sam as to the cause of the storm. Stealing was bad enough anyway, but on a Sunday!

Meanwhile, the lightning kept up its play. The thunder made talking arduous, but no one was anyhow in a mood to chatter. Only thunder was heard, and the hammering of the rain. But suddenly, close under the window, there burst out the most appalling inhuman shriek of terror.

"Tabby!" cried John, and they all rushed to the window.

But Tabby had already flashed into the house: and behind him was a whole club of wild cats in hot pursuit. John momentarily opened the dining-room door and puss slipped in, disheveled and panting. Not even then did the brutes desist: what insane fury led these jungle creatures to pursue him into the very house is unimaginable; but there they were, in the passage, caterwauling in concert: and as if at their incantation the thunder awoke anew, and the lightning nullified the meager table lamp. It was such a din as you could not speak through. Tabby, his fur on end, pranced up and down the room, his eyes blazing, talking and sometimes exclaiming in a tone of voice the children had never heard him use before and which made their blood run cold. He seemed like one inspired in the presence of Death, he had gone utterly Delphic: and without in the passage Hell's pandemonium reigned terrifically.

The check could only be a short one. Outside the door stood the big filter, and above the door the fanlight was long since broken. Something black and yelling flashed through the fanlight, landing clean in the middle of the supper table, scattering the forks and spoons and upsetting the lamp. And another and another—but already Tabby was through the window and streaking again for the bush. The whole dozen of those wild cats leapt one after the other from the top of the filter clean through the fanlight onto the supper table, and away from there only too hot in his tracks: in a moment the whole devil-hunt and its hopeless quarry had vanished into the night.

"Oh Tabby, my darling Tabby!" wailed John; while Emily rushed again to the window.

They were gone. The lightning behind the creepers in the jungle lit them up like giant cobwebs: but of Tabby and his pursuers there was nothing to be seen.

John burst into tears, the first time for several years, and flung himself on his mother: Emily stood transfixed at the window, her eyes glued in horror on what she could not, in fact, see: and all of a sudden was sick.

"God, what an evening!" groaned Mr. Bas-Thornton, groping in the darkness for what might be left of their supper.

Shortly after that Sam's hut burst into flames. They saw, from the dining-room, the old negro stagger dramatically out into the darkness. He was throwing stones at the sky. In a lull they heard him cry: "I gib it back, didn't I? I gib de nasty t'ing back?"

Then there was another blinding flash, and Sam fell where he stood. Mr. Thornton pulled the children roughly back and said something like "I'll go and see. Keep them from the window."

Then he closed and barred the shutters, and was gone.

John and the little ones kept up a continuous sobbing. Emily wished some one would light a lamp, she wanted to read. Anything, so as not to think about poor Tabby.

I suppose the wind must have begun to rise some while before this, but now, by the time Mr. Thornton had managed to carry old Sam's body into the house, it was more than a gale. The old man, stiff in the joints as he might have been in life, had gone as limp as a worm. Emily and John, who had slipped unbeknownst into the passage, were thrilled beyond measure at the way he dangled: they could hardly tear themselves away, and be back in the dining-room, before they should be discovered.

There Mrs. Thornton sat heroically in a chair, her brood all grouped round her, saying the Psalms, and the poems of Sir Walter Scott, over by heart: while Emily tried to keep her mind off Tabby by going over in her head all the details of her Earthquake. At times the din, the rocketing of the thunder and torrential shriek of the wind, became so loud as almost to impinge on her inner world: she wished this wretched thunderstorm would hurry up and get over. First she held an actual performance of the earthquake, went over it direct, as if it was again happening. Then she put it into Oratio Recta, told it as a story, beginning with that magic phrase, "Once I was in an Earthquake." But before long the dramatic element reappeared—this time, the awed comments of her imaginary English audience. When that was done, she put it into the Historical—a Voice, declaring that a girl called Emily was once in an Earthquake. And so on, right through the whole thing a third time.

The horrid fate of poor Tabby appeared suddenly before her eyes, caught her unawares: and she was all but sick again. Even her earthquake had failed her. Caught by the incubus, her mind struggled frantically to clutch at even the outside world, as an only remaining straw. She tried to fix her interest on every least detail of the scene around her—to count the slats in the shutters, any least detail that was *outward*. So it was that for the first time she really began to notice the weather.

The wind by now was more than redoubled. The shutters were bulging as if tired elephants were leaning against them, and Father was trying to tie the fastening with that handkerchief. But to push against this wind was like pushing against rock. The handkerchief, shutters, everything burst: the rain poured in like the sea into a sinking ship, the wind occupied the room, snatching pictures from the wall, sweeping the table bare. Through the gaping frames the lightning-lit scene without was visible. The creepers, which before had looked like cobwebs, now streamed up into the sky like new-combed hair. Bushes were lying flat, laid back on the ground as close as a rabbit lays back his ears. Branches were leaping about loose in the sky. The negro huts were clean gone, and the negroes crawling on their stomachs across the compound to gain the shelter of the house. The bouncing rain seemed to cover the ground with a white smoke, a sort of sea in which the blacks wallowed like porpoises. One nigger-boy began to roll away: his mother, forgetting caution, rose to her feet: and immediately the fat old beldam was blown clean away, bowling along across fields and hedge-rows like some one in a funny fairy-story, till she fetched up against a wall and was pinned there, unable to move. But the others managed to reach the house, and soon could be heard in the cellar underneath.

Moreover the very floor began to ripple, as a loose car-pet will ripple on a gusty day: in opening the cellar door the blacks had let the wind in, and now for some time they could not shut it again. The wind, to push against, was more like a solid block than a current of air.

Mr. Thornton went round the house—to see what could be done, he said. He soon realized that the next thing to go would be the roof. So he returned to the Niobe-group in the dining-room. Mrs. Thornton was half-way through *The Lady of the Lake*, the smaller chil-dren listening with rapt attention. Exasperated, he told them that they would probably not be alive in half an hour. No one seemed particularly interested in his news: Mrs. Thornton continued her recitation with faultless memory.

After another couple of cantos the threatened roof went. Fortunately, the wind taking it from inside, most of it was blown clear of the house: but one of the couples collapsed skew-eyed, and was hung up on what was left of the dining-room door—within an ace of hitting John. Emily, to her intense resentment, suddenly felt cold. All at once, she found she had had enough of the storm: it had become intolerable, instead of a welcome distraction.

Mr. Thornton began to look for something to break through the floor. If only he could make a hole in it, he might get his wife and children down into the cellar. Fortunately he did not have to look far: one arm of the fallen couple had already done the work for him. Laura, Rachel, Emily, Edward and John, Mrs. Thornton and finally Mr. Thornton himself, were passed down into the darkness already thronged with negroes and goats.

With great good sense, Mr. Thornton brought with him from the room above a couple of decanters of madeira, and every one had a swig, from Laura to the oldest negro. All the children made the most of this unholy chance, but somehow to Emily the bottle got passed twice, and each time she took a good pull. It was enough, at their age; and while what was left of the house was blown away over their heads, through the lull and the ensuing aerial return match, John, Emily, Edward, Rachel, and Laura, blind drunk, slept in a heap on the cellar floor: a sleep over which the appalling fate of Tabby, torn to pieces by those fiends almost under their very eyes, dominated with the easy empire of nightmare.

2

ALL NIGHT THE water poured through the house floor onto the people sheltering below: but (perhaps owing to the madeira) it did them no harm. Shortly after the second bout of blowing, however, the rain stopped; and when dawn came Mr. Thornton crept out to assess the damage.

The country was quite unrecognizable, as if it had been swept by a spate. You could hardly tell, geographically speaking, where you were. It is vegetation which gives the character to a tropic landscape, not the shape of the ground: and all the vegetation, for miles, was now pulp. The ground itself had been plowed up by instantaneous rivers, biting deep into the red earth. The only living thing in sight was a cow: and she had lost both her horns.

The wooden part of the house was nearly all gone.

After they had succeeded in reaching shelter, one wall after another had blown down. The furniture was splintered into matchwood. Even the heavy mahogany dining-table, which they loved, and had always kept with its legs in little glass baths of oil to defeat the ants, was spirited right away. There were some fragments which might be part of it, or they might not: you could not tell.

Mr. Thornton returned to the cellar and helped his wife out: she was so cramped as hardly to be able to move. They knelt down together and thanked God for not having treated them any worse. Then they stood up and stared about them rather stupidly. It seemed not credible that all this had been done by a current of air. Mr. Thornton patted the atmosphere with his hand. When still, it was so soft, so rare: how could one believe that Motion, itself something impalpable, had lent it a hardness: that this gentle, hind-like Meteor should have last night seized Fat Betsy with the rapacity of a tiger and the lift of a roc, and flung her, as he had seen her flung, across two fair-sized fields?

Mrs. Thornton understood his gesture.

"Remember who is its Prince," she said.

The stable was damaged, though not completely destroyed: and Mr. Thornton's mule was so much hurt he had to tell a negro to cut its throat. The buggy was smashed beyond repair. The only building undamaged was a stone chamber which had been the hospital of the old sugar-estate: so they woke the children, who were feeling ill and beyond words unhappy, and moved into this: where the negroes, with an unexpected energy and kindliness, did everything they could to make them comfortable. It was paved and unlighted: but solid.

The children were bilious for a few days, and inclined to dislike each other: but they accepted the change in their lives practically without noticing it. It is a fact that it takes experience before one can realize what is a catastrophe and what is not. Children have little faculty of distinguishing between disaster and the ordinary course of their lives. If Emily had known this was a *Hurricane*, she would doubt-less have been far more impressed, for the word was full of romantic terrors. But it never entered her head: and a thunderstorm, however severe, is after all a commonplace affair. The mere fact that it had done incalculable damage, while the earthquake had done none at all, gave it no right whatever to rival the latter in the hierarchy of cataclysms: an Earthquake is a thing apart. If she was silent, and in-clined to brood over some inward terror, it was not the hurricane she was thinking of, it was the death of Tabby. That, at times, seemed a horror beyond all bearing. It was her first intimate contact with death—and a death of violence, too. The death of Old Sam had no such effect: there is, after all, a vast difference between a negro and a favorite cat.

There was something enjoyable, too, in camping in the hospital: a sort of everlasting picnic in which their parents for once were taking part. Indeed it led them to begin for the first time to regard their parents as rational human beings, with understandable tastes—such as sitting on the floor to eat one's dinner.

It would have surprised Mrs. Thornton very much to have been told that hitherto she had meant practically nothing to her children. She took a keen interest in Psychology (the Art Babblative, Southey calls it). She was full of theories about their upbringing which she had not time to put into effect; but nevertheless she thought she had a deep understanding of their temperaments and was the center of their passionate devotion. Actually, she was congenitally incapable of telling one end of a child from the other. She was a dumpy little woman— Cornish, I believe. When she was herself a baby she was so small they carried her about on a cushion for fear a clumsy human arm might damage her. She could read when she was two and a half. Her reading was always serious. Nor had she been backward in the humaner studies: her mistresses spoke of her Deportment as something rarely seen outside the older Royal Houses: in spite of a figure like a bolster, she could step into a coach like an angel getting onto a cloud. She was very quick-tempered.

Mr. Bas-Thornton also had every accomplishment, except two: that of primogeniture, and that of making a living. Either would have provided for them.

If it would have surprised the mother, it would undoubtedly have surprised the children also to be told how
little their parents meant to them. Children seldom have
any power of quantitative self-analysis: whatever the
facts, they believe as an article of faith that they love
Father and Mother first and equally. Actually, the
Thornton children had loved Tabby first and foremost in
all the world, some of each other second, and hardly noticed their mother's existence more than once a week.
Their father they loved a little more: partly owing to the
ceremony of riding home on his stirrups.

Jamaica remained, and blossomed anew, its womb being
inexhaustible. Mr. and Mrs. Thornton remained, and with
patience and tears tried to reconstruct things, in so far as
they could be reconstructed. But the danger which their
beloved little ones had been through was not a thing to risk
again. Heaven had warned them. The children must go.

Nor was the only danger physical.

"That awful night!" said Mrs. Thornton, once, when
discussing their plan of sending them home to school:
"Oh my dear, what the poor little things must have suffered! Think how much more acute Fear is to a child! And
they were so brave, so English."

"I don't believe they realized it." (He only said that to be contradictious: he could hardly expect it to be taken seriously.)

"You know, I am terribly afraid what permanent, *inward* effect a shock like that may have on them. Have you noticed they never so much as mention it? In England they would at least be safe from dangers of that sort."

Meanwhile the children, accepting the new life as a matter of course, were thoroughly enjoying it. Most children, on a railway journey, prefer to change at as many stations as possible.

The rebuilding of Ferndale, too, was a matter of absorbing interest. For there is one advantage to these match-box houses—easy gone, easy come: and once begun, the work proceeded apace. Mr. Thornton himself led the building gang, employing no end of mechanical devices of his own devising, and it was not long before the day came when he stood with his handsome head emerging through the fast dwindling hole in the new roof, shouting directions to the two black carpenters, who, lying spread-eagle in their check shirts, pinned on shingle after shingle—walling him in, like the victim in some horrid story. At last he had to draw in his head, and where it had been the last few shingles were clapped into place.

An hour later the children had looked their last on Ferndale.

When they had been told they were to go to England, they had received it as an isolated fact: thrilling in itself, but without any particular causation—for it could hardly be due to the death of the cat, and nothing else of importance had occurred lately.

The first stage of their journey was by land, to Montego Bay, and the notable thing about it was that the borrowed wagonette was drawn not by a pair of horses or a pair of mules, but by one horse and one mule. Whenever the horse wanted to go fast the mule fell asleep in the shafts: and if the driver woke it up it set off at a gallop, which angered the horse. Their progress would have been slow anyhow, as all the roads were washed away.

John was the only one who could remember England. What he remembered was sitting at the top of a flight of stairs, which was fenced off from him by a little gate, playing with a red toy milk-cart: and he knew, without having to look, that in the room on the left Baby Emily was lying in her cot. Emily *said* she could remember something which sounded like a Prospect of the Backs of some Brick Houses at Richmond: but she might have invented it. The others had been born in the Island—Edward only just.

They all had, nevertheless, most elaborate ideas about England, built up out of what their parents had told them, and from the books and old magazines they sometimes looked at. Needless to say it was a very Atlantis, a land at the back of the North Wind: and going there was about as exciting as it would be to die and go to Heaven.

John told them all about the top of the stairs for the hundredth time as they drove along; the others listening attentively (as the Believing do to a man remembering his reincarnations).

Suddenly Emily recalled sitting at a window and seeing a big bird with a beautiful tail. At the same time there had been a horrid screeching going on, or perhaps something else disagreeable—she could not quite remember which sense was offended. It did not occur to her that it was this self-same bird which had screeched: and anyhow it was all too vague for her to try to describe it. She switched off to wondering how it was possible actually to *sleep* when walking, as the driver said the mule did.

They put up for the first night at St. Anne's, and there another notable thing occurred. Their host was a hardened Creole: and at supper he ate Cayenne pepper with a spoon. Not ordinary Cayenne pepper, mind, such as is sold in shops, which is heavily adulterated with logwood: but the far fierier pure original. This indeed was an Event of the first water: none of them ever forgot it.

The desolation through which they drove is indescribable. Tropical scenery is anyhow tedious, prolific, and gross: the greens more or less uniform: great tubular stems supporting thick leaves: no tree has an outline because it is crushed up against something else—no *room*. In Jamaica this profusion swarms over the very mountain ranges: and even the peaks are so numerous that on the top of one you are surrounded by others, and can see nothing. There are hundreds of flowers. Then imagine all this luxuriance smashed, as with a pestle and mortar—crushed, pulped, and already growing again! Mr. Thornton and his wife were ready to shout with relief when they caught their first glimpse of the sea, and at last came out in view of the whole beautiful sweep of Montego Bay itself.

In the open sea there was a considerable swell: but within the shelter of the coral reef, with its pinhole entrance, all was still as a mirror, where three ships of different sizes lay at anchor, the whole of each beautiful machine repeated in the water under it. Within the Roads lay the Bogue Islands; and immediately to the left of the islands, in the low land at the base of the hills, was the mouth of a small river—swampy, and (Mr. Thornton informed John) infested with crocodiles. The children had never seen a crocodile, and hoped one might venture as far as the town, where they presently arrived: but none did. It was with considerable disappointment that they found they were to go on board the barque at once; for they still hoped that round some corner of the street a crocodile might yet appear.

The *Clorinda* had let go her anchor in six fathoms: the water so clear, and the light so bright, that as they drew near the reflection suddenly disappeared, and instead they found themselves looking right underneath her and out the other side. The refraction made her seem as flat-bellied as a turtle, as if practically all of her were above the surface: and the anchor on its cable seemed to stream out flatly, like a downwards kite, twisting and twining (owing to the undulating surface) in the writhing coral.

This was the only impression Emily retained of going on board the ship: but the ship itself was a strange enough object, requiring all her attention. John was the only one who could remember the journey out at all clearly. Emily thought she could, but was really only remembering her visualizations of what she had been told: in fact, she found that a real ship was totally unlike the thing she thought she remembered.

By some last whim of the captain's the shrouds were being set up—tauter than seemed good to the sailors, who grumbled as they strained the creaking lanyards. John did not envy them, winding away at that handle in the hot sun: but he did envy the chap whose job it was to dip his hand in a great pot of aromatic Stockholm tar, and work it into the dead-eyes. He was tarred up to the elbows: and John itched to be so too.

In a moment the children were scattered all over the ship, smelling here, meowing, sniffing there, like cats in a new home. Mr. and Mrs. Thornton stood by the main companion-way, a little disconsolate at their children's happy preoccupation, a little regretting the lack of proper emotional scene.

"I think they will be happy here, Frederic," said Mrs. Thornton. "I wish we could have afforded to send them by the steam-boat: but children find amusement even in discomfort."

Mr. Thornton grunted.

"I wish schools had never been invented!" he suddenly burst out: "they wouldn't then be so indispensable!"

There was a short pause for the logic of this to cross the footlights: then he went on:

"I know what will happen; they'll come away . . . *mugs*! Just ordinary little mugs, like any one else's brats! I'm dashed if I don't think a hundred hurricanes would be better than that."

Mrs. Thornton shuddered: but she continued bravely:

"You know, I think they were getting almost *too* devoted to us? We have been such an unrivaled center of their lives and thoughts. It doesn't do for minds developing to be completely dependent on one person."

Captain Marpole's grizzled head emerged from the scuttle. A sea-dog: clear blue eyes of a translucent trustworthiness: a merry, wrinkled, morocco-colored face: a rumbling voice.

"He's too good to be true," whispered Mrs. Thornton.

"Not at all! It's a sophism to imagine people don't conform to type!" barked Mr. Thornton. He felt at sixes and sevens.

Captain Marpole certainly looked the ideal Children's Captain. He would, Mrs. Thornton decided, be careful without being fussy—for she was all in favor of courageous gymnastics, though glad she would not have to witness them herself. Captain Marpole cast his eyes benignantly over the swarming imps.

"They'll worship him," she whispered to her husband. (She meant, of course, that he would worship them.) It was an important point, this, of the captain: important as the personality of a headmaster.

"So that's the nursery, eh?" said the captain, crushing Mrs. Thornton's hand. She strove to answer, but found her throat undoubtedly paralyzed. Even Mr. Thornton's ready tongue was at a loss. He looked hard at the captain, jerked his thumb towards the children, wrestled in his mind with an elaborate speech, and finally enunciated in a small, unlikely voice:

"Smack 'em."

Then the captain had to go about his duties: and for an hour the father and mother sat disconsolately on the main hatch, quite deserted. Even when all was ready for departure it was impossible to muster the flock for a collective good-bye.

Already the tug was fulminating in its gorge: and ashore they must go. Emily and John had been captured, and stood talking uneasily to their parents, as if to strangers, using only a quarter of their minds. With a rope to be climbed dangling before his very nose, John simply did not know how this delay was to be supported, and lapsed into complete silence.

"Time to go ashore, Ma'am," said the captain: "we must be off now."

Very formally the two generations kissed each other, and said farewell. Indeed the elders were already at the gangway before the meaning of it all dawned in Emily's head. She rushed after her mother, gripped her ample flesh in two strong fists, and sobbed and wept, "Come too, Mother, oh, do come too!"

Honestly, it had only occurred to her that very moment that this was a *parting*.

"But think what an adventure it will be," said Mrs. Thornton bravely: "much more than if I came too!—You'll have to look after the Liddlies just as if you were a real grown-up!"

"But I don't want any more adventures!" sobbed Emily: "I've *got* an *Earthquake*!"

Passions were running far too high for any one to be aware how the final separation took place. The next thing Mrs. Thornton could remember was how tired her arm had been, after waving and waving at that dwindling speck which bore away on the land breeze, hung a while stationary in the intervening calm, then won the Trade and climbed up into the blue.

Meanwhile, at the rail stood Margaret Fernandez, who, with her little brother Harry, was going to England by the same boat. No one had come to see them off: and the brown nurse who was accompanying them had gone below the moment she came on board, so as to be ill as quickly as possible. How handsome Mr. Bas-Thornton had looked, with his English distinction! Yet every one knew he had no money. Her set white face was turned towards the land, her chin quivering at intervals. Slowly the harbor disappeared: the disordered profligacy of the turbulent, intricate mass of hills sunk lower in the sky. The occasional white houses, and white puffs of steam and smoke from the sugar-mills, vanished. At last the land, all palely shimmering like the bloom on grapes, settled down into the mirror of emerald and blue.

She wondered whether the Thornton children would prove companionable, or a nuisance. They were all younger than she was: which was a pity.

II

On the journey back to Ferndale both father and mother were silent, actuated by that tug of jealousy against sympathy which a strong common emotion begets in familiar rather than passionate companions. They were above the ordinary sentimentalities of grass-bereavement (above choking over small shoes found in cupboards): but not above a rather strong dose of the natural instincts of parenthood, Frederic no less than his wife.

But when they were nearly home, Mrs. Thornton began to chuckle to herself.

"Funny little thing, Emily! Did you notice almost the last thing she said? She said 'I've got an earthquake.' She must have got it mixed up in her silly old head with earache."

There was a long pause: and then she remarked again:

"John is so much the most sensitive: he was absolutely too full to speak."

III

When they got home it was many days before they could bring themselves openly to mention the children. When some reference had to be made, they spoke round them, in an uncomfortable way, as if they had died.

But after a few weeks they had a most welcome surprise. The *Clorinda* was calling at the Caymans, and taking the Leeward Passage: and while riding off the Grand Cayman Emily and John wrote letters, and a vessel bound for Kingston had taken charge of them and eventually they reached Ferndale. It had not even occurred to either parent that this would be possible.

This was Emily's:

> MY DEAR PARENTS,—This ship is full of Turtles. We stopped here and they came out in boats. There is turtles in the saloon under the tables for you to put your feet on, and turtles in the passages and on the deck, and everywhere you go. The captain says we mustn't fall overboard now because his boats are full of turtles too, with water. The sailors bring the others on deck every day to have a wash and when you stand them up they look just as if they had pinafores on. They make such a funny sighing and groaning in the night, at first I thought it was everybody being ill, but you get used to it, it is just like people being ill.—Your loving daughter,
>
> EMILY.

And John's:

MY DEAREST PARENTS,—The captain's son Henry is a
wonderful chap, he goes up the rigging with his
hands alone, he is ever so strong. He can turn round
under a bellying pin without touching the deck, I
can't but I hang from the ratlines by my heels which
the sailors say is very brave, but they don't like
Emily doing it, funny. I hope you are both in excellent health, one of the sailors has a monkey but its
tail is Sore.—Your affectionate Son,

JOHN.

That was the last news they could expect for many
months. The *Clorinda* was not touching anywhere else.
It gave Mrs. Thornton a cold feeling in the stomach to
measure just *how* long. But she argued, logically enough,
that the time must come to an end, all time does: there is
nothing so inexorable as a ship, plodding away, plodding
away, all over the place, till at last it quite certainly
reaches that small speck on the map which all the time
it had intended to reach. Philosophically speaking, a ship
in its port of departure is just as much in its port of arrival: two point-events differing in time and place, but
not in degree of reality. *Ergo*, that first letter from

England was as good as written, only not quite . . . legible yet. And the same applied to seeing them. (But here one must stop, for the same argument applied to old age and death, it wouldn't do.)

Yet, a bare fortnight after the arrival of this first budget, still another letter arrived, from Havana. The *Clorinda* had put in there unexpectedly, it appeared: the letter was from Captain Marpole.

"What a dear man he is," said Alice. "He must have known how anxious we would be for every scrap of news."

Captain Marpole's letter was not so terse and vivid as the children's had been: still, for the news it contained, I give it in full:

HAVANA DE CUBA.

HONORED SIR AND MADAM,—I hasten to write to you to relieve you of any uncertainty!

After leaving the Caymans we stood for the Leeward Passage, and sighted the Isle of Pines and False Cape on the morning of the 19th and Cape S. Antonio in the evening, but were prevented from rounding the same by a true Norther, the first of the season, on the 22nd, however, the wind coming round sufficiently we rounded the cape in a lively fashion and stood $N\frac{1}{2}E$. well away from the Coloradoes which are a dangerous reef lying off this part of the Cuban coast. At six o'clock on the morning of the 23rd there being light airs only I sighted three sail in the North-East, evidently merchantmen bound on the same course as ourselves, at the same time a schooner of similar character was observed standing out towards us from the direction of Black Key, and I pointed her out to my mate just before going below, having the wind of us he was within hailing distance by ten in the morning, judge then of our astonishment when he rudely opened ten or twelve disguised gun-ports and unmasked a whole broadside of artillery trained upon us, ordering us at the same time in the most peremptory manner to heave-to or he would sink us instanter. There was nothing to do but to comply although considering the friendly relations at present existing between the English and all other governments my mate was quite at a loss to account for his action, and imagined it due to a mistake which would be speedily explained, we were immediately boarded by about fifty or seventy ruffians of the worst Spanish type, armed with knives and cutlasses, who took possession of the ship and confined me in my cabin and my mate and crew forward while they ransacked the vessel committing every possible excess broach-

ing rum-casks and breaking the necks off wine-
bottles and soon a great number of them were lying
about the deck in an intoxicated condition, their
leader then informed me he was aware I had a considerable sum in specie on board and used *every
possible threat which villainy could devise* to make
me disclose its hiding-place, it was useless for me to
asure him that beyond the fifty or so pounds they
had already discovered I carried none, he grew even
more insistent in his demands, declaring that his information was certain, tearing down the paneling
in my cabin in his search. He carried off my instruments, my clothes, and all my personal possessions,
even taking from me the poor Locket in which I was
used to carry the portrait of my Wife, and no appeal
to his sensibility, tho' I shed tears, would make him
return this to him worthless object, he also tore
down and carried away the cabin bell-pulls, which
could be of no possible use to him and was an act of
the most open *piracy*, at length, seeing I was obdu-
rate, he threatened to blow up the ship *and all in it*
if I would not yield, he prepared the train and would
have proceeded to carry out this devilish threat if I
had not in this last extremity, consented.

I come now to the latter part of my tale. The children had taken refuge in the deck-house and had

been up to now free from harm, except for a cuff or two and the Degrading Sights they must have witnessed, but no sooner was the specie some five thousand pounds in all mostly my private property and most of our cargo (chiefly rum sugar coffee and arrowroot) removed to the schooner than her captain, in sheer infamous wantonness, had them all brought out from their refuge your own little ones and the two Fernandez children who were also on board and murdered them, every one. That anything so wicked should look like a man I should not have believed, had I been told, tho' I have lived long and seen all kinds of men, I think he is mad: indeed I am sure of it; and I take Oath that he shall be brought to at least that tithe of justice which is in Human hands, for two days we drifted about in a helpless condition, for our rigging had all been cut, and at last fell in with an American man-of-war, who gave us some assistance, and would have proceeded in pursuit of the miscreants himself had he not most explicit orders to elsewhere. I then put in to the port of Havana, where I informed the correspondent of Lloyds, the government, and the representative of the *Times* newspaper, and take the opportunity of writing you this melancholy letter before proceeding to England.

There is one point on which you will still feel some anxiety, considering the sex of some of the poor innocents, and on which I am glad to be able to set your minds at rest, the children were taken onto the other vessel in the evening and I am glad to say there done to death *immediately*, and their little bodies cast into the sea, as I saw with great relief with my own eyes. There was no time for what you might fear to have occurred, and this consolation I am glad to be able to give you.—I have the honor to be,

Your obedient servant,

JAS. MARPOLE,

Master, barque *Clorinda*.

3

THE PASSAGE FROM Montego Bay to the Caymans, where the children had written their letters, is only a matter of a few hours: indeed, in clear weather one can look right across from Jamaica to the peak of Tarquinio in Cuba.

There is no harbor; and the anchorage, owing to the reefs and ledges, is difficult. The *Clorinda* brought up off the Grand Cayman, the look-out man in the chains feeling his way to a white, sandy patch of bottom which affords the only safe resting-place there, and causing the anchor to be let go to windward of it. Luckily, the weather was fine.

The island, a longish one at the western end of the group, is low, and covered with palms. Presently a succession of boats brought out a quantity of turtles, as

Emily described. The natives also brought parrots to sell to the sailors: but failed to dispose of many.

At last, however, the uncomfortable Caymans were left behind, and they set their course towards the Isle of Pines, a large island in a gulf of the Cuban coast. One of the sailors, called Curtis, had once been wrecked there, and was full of stories about it. It is a very unpleasant place; sparsely inhabited, and covered with labyrinthine woods. The only food available is a kind of tree. There is also a species of bean which looks tempting: but it is deadly poison. The crocodiles, Curtis said, were so fierce they chased him and his companions into trees: the only way to escape from them was to throw them your cap to worry: or if you were bold, to disable them with a blow of a stick on the loins. There were also a great many snakes, including a kind of boa.

The current off the Isle of Pines sets strongly to the east: so the *Clorinda* kept close inshore, to cheat it. They passed Cape Corrientes—looking, when first sighted, like two hummocks in the sea: they passed Holandes Point, known as False C. Antonio: but were prevented for some time, as Captain Marpole told in his letter, from rounding the true one. For to attempt C. Antonio in a Norther is to waste your labor.

They lay-to in sight of that long, low, rocky, treeless promontory in which the great island of Cuba terminates, and waited. They were so close that the fisher-man's hut on its southern side was clearly discernible.

For the children, those first few days at sea had flashed by like a kind of prolonged circus. There is no machine invented for sober purposes so well adapted also to play as the rigging of a ship: and the kindly captain, as Mrs. Thorn-ton had divined, was willing to give them a lot of freedom. First came the climbing of a few rungs of the ratlines in a sailor's charge: higher each time, till John attained a gin-gerly touching of the yard: then hugged it: then straddled it. Soon, running up the ratlines and prancing on the yard (as if it were a mere table-top) had no further thrill for John or Emily either. (To go out on the yard was not allowed.)

But when the ratlines had palled, the most lasting joy undoubtedly lay in that network of footropes and chains and stays which spreads out under and on each side of the bowsprit. Here, familiarity only bred content. Here, in fine weather, one could climb or be still: stand, sit, hang, swing, or lie: now this end up, now that: and all with the cream of the blue sea being whipt up for one's own especial pleasure, almost within touching distance: and the big white wooden lady (Clorinda herself), bearing the whole vessel so lightly on her back, her knees in the hubble-bubble, her cracks almost filled up with so much painting, vaster than any living lady, as a constant and unannoying companion.

In the midst there was a kind of spear, its haft set against the under-side of the bowsprit, its point perpendicularly down towards the water—the dolphin-striker. Here it was that the old monkey (who had the Sore tail) loved to hang, by the mere stub which was all a devouring cancer had left him, chattering to the water. He took no notice of the children, nor they of him: but both parties grew attached to each other, for all that.

—How small the children all looked, on a ship, when you saw them beside the sailors! It was as if they were a different order of beings! Yet they were living creatures just the same, full of promise.

John, with his downy, freckled face, and general round energeticalness.

Emily, with her huge palm-leaf hat, and colorless cotton frock tight over her minute impish erect body: her thin, almost expressionless face: her dark gray eyes contracted to escape the blaze, yet shining as it were in spite of themselves: and her really beautiful lips, that looked almost as if they were sculptured.

Margaret Fernandez, taller (as midgets go: she was just thirteen), with her square white face and tangled hair, her elaboratish clothes.

Her little brother *Harry*, by some throw-back for all the world like a manikin Spaniard.

And the smaller Thorntons: *Edward*, mouse-colored,

with a general mousy (but pleasing) expression: *Rachel*, with tight short gold curls and a fat pink face (John's coloring watered down): and last of all *Laura*, a queer mite of three with heavy dark eyebrows, and blue eyes, a big head-top and a receding chin—as if the Procreative Spirit was getting a little hysterical by the time it reached her. A silver-age conception, Laura's, decidedly.

When the Norther blew itself out, it soon fell away almost dead calm. The morning they finally rounded Cape San Antonio was hot, blazing hot. But it is never stuffy at sea: there is only this disadvantage, that while on land a shady hat protects you from the sun, at sea nothing can protect you from that second sun which is mirrored upwards from the water, strikes under all defenses, and burns the unseasoned skin from all your undersides. Poor John! His throat and chin were a blistered red.

From the point itself there is a whitish bank in two fathoms, bowed from north to north-east. The outer side is clean and steep-to, and in fine weather one can steer along it by eye. It ends in Black Key, a rock standing out of the water like a ship's hull. Beyond that lies a channel, very foul and difficult to navigate: and beyond that again the Coloradoes Reef begins, the first of a long chain of reefs following the coast in a north-easterly direction as far as Honde Bay, two-thirds the way to Havana. Within the reefs lies the intricate Canal de Guaniguanico, of which this channel is the westernmost outlet, with its own rather dubious little ports. But ocean traffic, needless to say, shuns the whole box of tricks: and the *Clorinda* advisedly stood well away to the northward, keeping her course at a gentle amble for the open Atlantic.

John was sitting outside the galley with the sailor called Curtis, who was instructing him in the neat mystery of a Turk's-head. Young Henry Marpole was steering. Emily was messing around—not talking, just being by him.

As for the other sailors, they were all congregated in a ring, up in the bows, so that one saw nothing but their backs. But every now and then a general guffaw, and a sudden surging of the whole group, showed they were up to something or other.

John presently tiptoed forward, to see what it might be. He thrust his bullet-head among their legs, and worked his way in till he had as good a view as the earliest comer.

He found they had got the old monkey, and were filling him up with rum. First they gave him biscuit soaked in it: then they dipped rags in a pannikin of the stuff, and squeezed them into his mouth. Then they tried to make him drink direct: but that he would not do—it only wasted a lot of spirit.

John felt a vague horror at all this: though of course he did not guess the purpose behind it.

The poor brute shivered and chattered, rolled his eyes, spluttered. I suppose it must have been an excruciatingly funny sight. Every now and then he would seem altogether overcome by the spirit. Then one of them would lay him on the top of an old beef barrel—but hey presto, he would be up like lightning, trying to streak through the air over their heads. But he was no bird: they caught him each time, and set to work to dope him again.

As for John, he could no more have left the scene now than Jacko the monkey could.

It was astonishing what a lot of spirit the wizened little brute could absorb. He was drunk, of course: hopelessly, blindly, madly drunk. But he was not paralytic, not even somnolent: and it seemed as if nothing could overcome him. So at last they gave up the attempt. They fetched a wooden box, and cut a notch in the edge. Then they put him on the barrel-top, and clapped the box over him, and after much maneuvering his gangrenous tail was made to come out through the notch. Anesthetized or not, the operation on him was to proceed. John stared, transfixed, at that obscene wriggling stump which was all one could see of the animal: and out of the corner of his eye he could see at the same time the uproarious operators, the tar-stained knife.

But the moment the blade touched flesh, with an awful screech the mommet contrived to fling off his cage—

leapt on the surgeon's head—leapt from there high in the air—caught the forestay—and in a twinkling was away and up high in the forerigging.

Then began the hue and cry. Sixteen men flinging about in lofty acrobatics, all to catch one poor old drunk monkey. For he was drunk as a lord, and sick as a cat. His course varied between wild and hair-raising leaps (a sort of inspired gymnastics), and doleful incompetent reelings on a taut rope which threatened at every moment to cat-apult him into the sea. But even so they could never quite catch him.

No wonder that all the children, now, stood open-mouthed and open-eyed on the deck beneath in the sun till their necks nearly broke—*such* a Free Fun Fair and Circus!

And no wonder that on that passenger-schooner which Marpole, before going below, had sighted drifting towards them from the direction of the Black Key channel, the ladies had left the shade of the awning and were crowding at the rail, parasols twirling, lorgnettes and opera-glasses in action, all twittering like a cage of linnets. Just too far off to distinguish the tiny quarry, they might well have wondered what sort of a bedlam-vessel of sea-acrobats the light easterly air was bearing them down upon.

They were so interested that presently a boat was hoisted out, and the ladies—and some gentlemen as well—crowded into it.

Poor little Jacko missed his hold at last: fell plump on the deck and broke his neck. That was the end of him—and of the hunt too, of course. The aerial ballet was over, in its middle, with no final tableau. The sailors began, in twos and threes, to slide to the deck.

But the visitors were already on board.

That is how the *Clorinda* really was taken. There was no display of artillery—but then, Captain Marpole could hardly know this, seeing he was below in his bunk at the time. Henry was steering by that sixth sense which only comes into operation when the other five are asleep. The mate and crew had been so intent on what they were doing that the Flying Dutchman himself might have laid alongside, for all they cared.

II

Indeed, the whole maneuver was executed so quietly that Captain Marpole never even woke—incredible though this will seem to a seaman. But then, Marpole had begun life as a successful coal-merchant.

The mate and crew were bundled into the fo'c'sle (the Fox-hole, the children thought it was called), and confined there, the scuttle being secured with a couple of nails.

The children themselves were shepherded, as related, into the deck-house, where the chairs, and perfectly useless pieces of old rope, and broken tools, and dried-up paint-pots were kept, without taking alarm. But the door was immediately shut on them. They had to wait for hours and hours before anything else happened—nearly all day, in fact: and they got very bored, and rather cross.

The actual number of the men who had effected the capture cannot have been more than eight or nine, most of them "women" at that, and not armed—at least with any visible weapon. But a second boatload soon followed them from the schooner. These, for form's sake, were armed with muskets. But there was no possible resistance to fear. Two long nails through the scuttle can secure any number of men pretty effectually.

With this second boatload came both the captain and the mate. The former was a clumsy great fellow, with a sad, silly face. He was bulky; yet so ill-proportioned one got no impression of power. He was modestly dressed in a drab shore-going suit: he was newly shaven, and his sparse hair was pomaded so that it lay in a few dark ribbons across his baldish head-top. But all this shore-decency of appearance only accentuated his big splodgy brown hands, stained and scarred and corned with his calling. Moreover, instead of boots he wore a pair of gigantic heel-less slippers in the Moorish manner, which he must have sliced with a knife out of some pair of dead sea-boots. Even his great spreading feet could hardly keep them on, so that he was obliged to walk at the slowest of shuffles, flop-flop along the deck. He stooped, as if always afraid of banging his head on something; and carried the backs of his hands forward, like an orangutan.

Meanwhile the men set to work methodically but very quietly to remove the wedges that held the battens of the hatches, getting ready to haul up the cargo.

Their leader took several turns up and down the deck before he seemed able to make up his mind to the interview: then lowered himself into Marpole's cabin, followed by his mate.

This mate was a small man: very fair, and intelligent-looking beside his chief. He was almost dapper, in a quiet way, in his dress.

They found Captain Marpole even now only half awake: and the stranger stood for a moment in silence, nervously twiddling his cap in his hands. When he spoke at last, it was with a soft German accent:

"Excuse me," he began, "but would you have the goodness to lend me a few stores?"

Captain Marpole stared in astonishment, first at him and then at the much be-painted faces of the "ladies" pressed against his cabin skylight.

"Who the devil are you?" he contrived to ask at last.

"I hold a commission in the Columbian navy," the stranger explained: "and I am in need of a few stores."

(Meanwhile his men had the hatches off, and were preparing to help themselves to everything in the ship.)

Marpole looked him up and down. It was barely conceivable that even the Columbian navy should have such a figure of an officer. Then his eye wandered back to the skylight:

"If you call yourself a man-of-war, sir, who in Heaven's name are *those*?" As he pointed, the smirking faces hastily retreated.

The stranger blushed.

"They are rather difficult to explain," he admitted ingenuously.

"If you had said *Turkish* navy, that would have been more reasonable-sounding!" said Marpole.

But the stranger did not seem to take the joke. He stood, silent, in a characteristic attitude: rocking himself from foot to foot, and rubbing his cheek on his shoulder.

Suddenly Marpole's ear caught the muffled racketing forward. Almost at the same time a bump that shivered the whole barque told that the schooner had been laid alongside.

"What's that?" he exclaimed. "Is there some one in my hold?"

"Stores . . ." mumbled the stranger.

Marpole up to now had lain growling in his bunk like a dog in its kennel. Now for the first time realizing that something serious was afoot he flung himself out and made for the companion-way. The little silent fair man tripped him up, and he fell against the table.

"You had much better stay here, yes?" said the big man. "My fellows shall keep a tally, you shall be paid in full for everything we take."

The eyes of the marine coal-merchant gleamed momentarily:

"You'll have to pay for this outrage to a pretty tune!" he growled.

"I will pay you," said the stranger, with a sudden magnificence in his voice, "at the very least five thousand pounds!"

Marpole stared in astonishment.

"I will write you an order on the Columbian government for that amount," the other went on.

Marpole thumped the table, almost speechless:

"D'you think I believe that cock-and-bull story?" he thundered.

Captain Jonsen made no protest.

"Do you realize that you are technically guilty of *piracy*, making a forced requisition on a British ship like this, even if you pay every farthing?"

Still Jonsen made no reply: though the bored expression of his mate was lit up for a moment by a smile.

"You'll pay me in *cash*!" Marpole concluded. Then he

went off on a fresh tack: "Though how the devil you got on board without being called beats me!—Where's my mate?"

Jonsen began in a toneless voice, as if by rote: "I will write you an order for five thousand pounds: three thousand for the stores, and two thousand you will give me in money."

"We know you've got specie on board," interjected the little fair mate, speaking for the first time.

"Our information is certain!" declared Jonsen.

Marpole at last went white and began to sweat. It took even Fear an extraordinarily long time to penetrate his thick skull. But he denied that he had any treasure on board.

"Is that your answer?" said Jonsen. He drew a heavy pistol from his side pocket. "If you do not tell us the truth, your life shall pay the forfeit." His voice was peculiarly gentle, and mechanical, as if he did not attach much meaning to what he said. "Do not expect mercy, for this is my profession, and in it I am inured to blood."

A frightful squawking from the deck above told Marpole that his chickens were being moved to new quarters.

In an agony of feeling Marpole told him that he had a wife and children, who would be left destitute if his life was taken.

Jonsen, with rather a perplexed look on his face, put the gun back in his pocket, and the two of them began to search for themselves, at the same time stripping the saloon and cabins of everything they contained: firearms, wearing apparel, the bedclothes, and even (as Marpole with a rare touch of accuracy mentioned in his report) the bell-pulls.

Overhead there was a continuous bumping: the rolling of casks, cases, etc.

"Remember," Jonsen went on over his shoulder while he searched, "money cannot recall life, nor in the least avail you when you are dead. If you regard your life in the least, at once acquaint me with the hiding-place, and your life shall be safe."

Marpole's only reply was again to invoke the thought of his wife and children (he was, as a matter of fact, a widower: and his only relative, a niece, would be the better off by his death to the tune of some ten thousand pounds).

But this reiteration seemed to give the mate an idea: and he began to talk to his chief rapidly in a language Marpole had never even heard. For a moment a curious glint came into Jonsen's eye: but soon he was chuckling in the sentimentalest manner, and rubbing his hands.

The mate went on deck to prepare things.

Marpole had no inkling of what was afoot. The mate went on deck to prepare his plan, whatever it was: and Jonsen busied himself with a last futile search for the hiding-place, in silence.

Presently the mate shouted down to him, and he ordered Marpole on deck.

Poor Marpole groaned. Unloading cargo is inclined to be a messy business any way: but these visitors had been none too careful. There is no smell in the world worse than when molasses and bilge-water marry: now it was let loose like ten thousand devils. His heart was almost broken when he saw the havoc that had been made with the cargo: broken cases, casks, bottles, all about the deck: everything in the greatest confusion: tarpaulins cut to pieces: hatches broken.

From the deck-house came the piercing voice of Laura: *"I want to come out!"*

The Spanish ladies seemed to have returned to the schooner. His own men were shut up in the fo'c'sle. It was obvious where all the children were, for Laura was not the only vociferator. But the only persons to be seen were six members of the visiting crew, who stood in a line, facing the deck-house, a musket apiece.

It was the little mate who now took charge of the situation:

"Where is your specie hid, Captain?"

The musketeers having their backs to him, "Go to the Devil!" replied Marpole.

A startling volley rang out: six neat holes were punctured in the top of the deck-house.

"Hi! Steady there, what are you doing?" John cried out indignantly from within.

"If you refuse to tell us, next time their aim will be a foot lower."

"You fiends!" cried Marpole.

"Will you tell me?"

"*No!*"

"*Fire!*"

The second row of holes can only have missed the taller children by a few inches.

There was a moment's silence: then a sudden wild shriek from within the deck-house. It was so terrified a sound not their own mothers could have told which throat it came from. One only, though.

The stranger-captain had been slouching about in an agitated way: but at that shriek he turned on Marpole, his face purple with a sudden fury:

"*Now* will you say?"

But Marpole was now completely master of himself. He did not hesitate:

"NO!"

"Next time he gives the order it will be to shoot right through their little bodies!"

So that was what Marpole had meant in his letter by "*every possible threat which villainy could devise*"! But even by this he was not to be daunted:

"No, I tell you!"

Heroic obstinacy! But instead of giving the fatal order, Jonsen lifted a paw like a bear's, and banged Marpole's jaw with it. The latter fell to the deck, stunned.

It was then they took the children out of the deck-house.

They were not really much frightened; except Margaret, who did seem to be taking it all to heart rather. Being shot at is so unlike what one expects it to be that one can hardly connect the two ideas enough to have the appropriate emotions, the first few times. It is not half so startling as some one jumping out on you with a "*Boo!*" in the dark, for instance. The boys were crying a little: the girls were hot and cross and hungry.

"What were you doing?" Rachel asked brightly of one of the firing-party.

But only the captain and the mate could speak English. The latter, ignoring Rachel's question explained that they were all to go on board the schooner—"to have some supper," he said.

He had all a sailor's reassuring charm of manner. So under the charge of two Spanish seamen they were helped over the bulwarks onto the smaller vessel, which was just casting off.

There the strange sailors broke open a whole case of crystallized fruits, on which they might turn the edge of their long appetites as much as they would.

WHEN POOR STUNNED Captain Marpole came to his senses, it was to find himself tied to the mainmast. Several handfuls of shavings and splintered wood were piled round his feet, and Jonsen was sprinkling them plentifully with gun-powder—though not perhaps enough, it is true, to "blow up the ship and all in it."

The small fair mate stood at hand in the gathering dusk with a lighted torch, ready to fire the pyre.

What could a man do in such straits? At that dreadful moment the gallant old fellow had to admit that he was beaten at last. He told them where his freight-money— some £900—was hidden: and they let him go.

Just as the darkness closed in, the last of the pirates returned to their ship. Not a sound was to be heard of the children: but Marpole guessed that they had been taken there too.

Before releasing his crew he lit a lantern and began a sort of inventory of what was gone. It was heart-breaking enough: besides the cargo, all his spare sails, cordage, provisions, guns, paint, powder: all his wearing apparel, and that of his mate: all nautical instruments gone, cabin stores—the saloon in fact gutted of everything, not even a knife or spoon left, tea or sugar, nor a second shirt to his back left. Only the children's luggage was left untouched: and the turtles. Their melancholy sighing was the sole sound to be heard.

But it was almost as heart-breaking to see what the pirates had *left*: anything damaged, such worn-out and useless gear as he had been only waiting for some "storm" to wash overboard—not one of these eyesores was missing.

What, in Heaven's name, was the use of an insurance policy? He began to collect the rubbish himself and dump it over the side.

But Captain Jonsen saw him:

"Hi!" he shouted: "You dirty svindler! I will write to Lloyds and expose you! I will write myself!" He was horribly shocked at the other's dishonesty.

So Marpole had to give it up, for the time at any rate: took a spike and broke open the fo'c'sle: and as well as the sailors found Margaret's brown nurse. She had hidden there the whole day: probably from motives of fright.

III

You would have thought that supper on the schooner that night would have been a hilarious affair. But, somehow, it was manqué.

A prize of such value had naturally put the crew in the best of humors: and a meal which consisted mainly of crystallized fruit, followed as an afterthought by bread and chopped onions served in one enormous communal bowl, eaten on the open deck under the stars, after bed-time, should have done the same by the children. But nevertheless both parties were seized by a sudden, overpowering, and most unexpected fit of shyness. Consequently no state banquet was ever so formal, or so boring.

I suppose it was the lack of a common language which first generated the infection. The Spanish sailors, used enough to this difficulty, grinned, pointed, and bobbed: but the children retired into a display of good manners which it would certainly have surprised their parents to see. Whereon the sailors became equally formal: and one poor monkeyfied little fellow who by nature belched continually was so be-nudged and be-winked by his companions, and so covered in confusion of his own accord, that presently he went away to eat by himself. Even then, so silent was this revel, he could still be heard faintly belching, half the ship's length away.

Perhaps it would have gone better if the captain and mate had been there, with their English. But they were too busy, looking over the personal belongings they had brought from the barque, sorting out by the light of a lantern anything too easily identifiable and reluctantly committing it to the sea.

It was at the loud splashes made by a couple of empty trunks, stamped in large letters JAS. MARPOLE, that a roar of unassumed indignation arose from the neighboring barque. The two paused in their work, astonished: why should a crew already spoiled of all they possessed take it so hardly when one heaved a couple of old worthless trunks in the sea?

It was inexplicable.

They continued their task, taking no further notice of the *Clorinda*.

Once supper was over, the social situation became even more awkward. The children stood about, not knowing what to do with their hands, or even their legs: unable to talk to their hosts, and feeling it would be rude to talk to each other, wishing badly that it was time to leave. If only it had been light they could have been happy enough exploring: but in the darkness there was nothing to do, nothing whatever.

The sailors soon found occupations of their own: and the captain and mate, as I have said, were already busy.

Once the sorting was over, however, there was nothing for Jonsen to do except return the children to the barque, and get well clear while the breeze and the darkness lasted.

But on hearing those splashes, Marpole's lively imagination had interpreted them in his own way. They suggested that there was now no reason to wait: indeed, every reason to be gone.

I think he was quite honestly misled.

It was after all but a small slip to say he had "seen with his own eyes" what he had heard with his own ears: and the intention was pious.

He set his men feverishly to work: and when Captain Jonsen looked his way again, the *Clorinda*, with every stitch spread in the starlight, was already half a mile to leeward.

To pursue her, right in the track of shipping, was out of the question. Jonsen had to content himself with staring after her through his nightglass.

IV

Captain Jonsen set the little monkeyfied sailor, who had been so mortified earlier in the evening, to clear the schooner's fore-hold. The warps and brooms and fenders it contained were all piled to one side, and a sufficiency of bedclothes for the guests was provided from the plunder.

But nothing could now thaw them. They clambered down the ladder and received their blanket apiece in an uncomfortable silence. Jonsen hung about, anxious to be helpful in this matter of getting into beds which were not there, but not knowing how to set about it. So he gave it up at last, and swung himself up through the fore-hatch, talking to himself.

The last they saw of him was his fantastic slippers, hanging each from a big toe, outlined against the stars: but it never entered their heads to laugh.

Once, however, the familiar comfort of a blanket under their chins had begun to have its effect, and they were obviously quite alone, a little life did begin to return into these dumb statues.

The darkness was profound, only accentuated by the starlit square of the open hatchway. First the long silence was broken by some one turning over, almost freely. Then presently:

LAURA (*in slow, sepulchral tones*). I don't like this bed.

RACHEL (*ditto*). I do.

LAURA. It's a horrid bed; there isn't any!

EMILY.
JOHN. } Sh! Go to sleep!

EDWARD. I smell cockroaches.

EMILY. Sh!

EDWARD (*loudly and hopefully*). They'll bite all our nails off, because we haven't washed, and our skin, and our hair, and—

LAURA. There's a cockroach in my bed! Get out!

(*You could hear the brute go zooming away. But Laura was already out too.*)

EMILY. Laura! Go back to bed!

LAURA. I can't when there's a cockroach in it!

JOHN. Get into bed again, you little fool! He's gone long ago!

LAURA. But I expect he has left his wife.

HARRY. They don't have wives, they're wives themselves.

RACHEL. Ow!—Laura, stop it!—Emily, Laura's walking on me!

EMILY. Lau-rer!

LAURA. Well, I must walk on something!

EMILY. Go to sleep!

(*Silence for a while.*)

LAURA. I haven't said my prayers.

EMILY. Well, say them lying down.

RACHEL. She mustn't, that's lazy.

JOHN. Shut up, Rachel, she must.

RACHEL. It's wicked! You go to sleep in the middle then. People who go to sleep in the middle ought to be damned, they ought.—Oughtn't they? (*Silence.*) Oughtn't they? (*Still silence.*) Emily, I say, oughtn't they?

JOHN. NO!

RACHEL (*dreamily*). I think there's lots more people ought to be damned than are.

(*Silence again.*)

HARRY. Marghie.

(*Silence.*)

Marghie!

(*Silence.*)

JOHN. What's up with Marghie? Won't she speak?

(*A faint sob is heard.*)

HARRY. I don't know.

(*Another sob.*)

JOHN. Is she often like this?

HARRY. She's an awful ass sometimes.

JOHN. Marghie, what's up?

MARGARET (*miserably*). Let me alone!

RACHEL. I believe she's frightened! (*Chants tauntingly*) Marghie's got the bogies, the bogies, the bogies!

MARGARET (*sobbing out loud*). *Oh* you little fools!

JOHN. Well, what's the matter with you, then?

MARGARET (*after a pause*). I'm older than any of you.

HARRY. Well, *that's* a funny reason to be frightened!

MARGARET. It isn't.

HARRY. It is!

MARGARET (*warming to the argument*). It isn't, I tell you!

HARRY. *It is!*

MARGARET (*smugly*). That's simply because you're all too young to know . . .

JOHN. Oh, hit her, Emily!

EMILY (*sleepily*). Hit her yourself.

HARRY. But, Marghie, why are we here?

(*No answer.*)

Emily, why are we here?

EMILY (*indifferently*). I don't know. I expect they just wanted to change us.

HARRY. I expect so. But they never *told* us we were going to be changed.

EMILY. Grown-ups never *do* tell us things.

4

THE CHILDREN ALL slept late, and all woke at the same moment as if by clockwork. They sat up, and yawned uniformly, and stretched the stiffness out of their legs and backs (they were lying on solid wood, remember).

The schooner was steady, and people tramping about the deck. The main-hold and fore-hold were all one: and from where they were they could see the main-hatch had been opened. The captain appeared through it legs first, and dropped onto the higgledy-piggledy of the *Clorinda*'s cargo.

For some time they simply stared at him. He looked uneasy, and was talking to himself as he tapped now this case with his pencil, now that; and presently shouted rather fiercely to people on deck.

"All right, all right," came from above the injured voice of the mate. "There's no such hurry as all that."

On which the captain's mutterings to himself swelled, as if ten people were conversing at once in his chest.

"May we get up yet?" asked Rachel.

Captain Jonsen spun round—he had forgotten their existence.

"Eh?"

"May we get up, please?"

"You can go to the debble." He muttered this so low the children did not hear it. But it was not lost on the mate.

"Hey! Ey! Ey!" he called down, reprovingly.

"Yes! Get up! Go on deck! Here!" The captain viciously set up a short ladder for them to climb through the hatch.

They were greatly astonished to find the schooner was no longer at sea. Instead, she was snugly moored against a little wooden wharf, in a pleasant land-locked bay; with a pleasant but untidy village, of white wooden houses with palm-leaf roofs, behind it; and the tower of a small sandstone church emerging from the abundant greenery. On the quay were a few well-dressed loungers, watching the preparations for unloading. The mate was directing the labors of the crew, who were rigging the cargo-gaff and getting ready for a hot morning's work.

The mate nodded cheerfully to the children, but thereafter took no notice of them, which was rather mortifying. The truth is that the man was busy.

At the same time there emerged from somewhere aft a collection of the oddest-looking young men. Margaret decided she had never seen such beautiful young men before. They were slim, yet nicely rounded: and dressed in exquisite clothes (if a trifle threadbare). But their faces! Those beautiful olive-tinted ovals! Those large, black-ringed, soft brown eyes, those unnaturally carmine lips! They minced across the deck, chattering to each other in high-pitched tones, "twittering like a cage of linnets . . ." and made their way on shore.

"Who are they?" Emily asked the captain, who had just re-emerged from below.

"Who are who?" he murmured absently, without looking round. "Oh, those? Fairies."

"*Hey! Yey! Yey!*" cried the mate, more disapprovingly than ever.

"*Fairies?*" cried Emily in astonishment.

But Captain Jonsen began to blush. He went crimson from the nape of his neck to the bald patches on the top of his head, and left.

"He is *silly!*" said Emily.

"I wonder if we go onto the land yet," said Edward.

"We'd better wait until we're told, hadn't we, Emily?" said Harry.

"I didn't know England would be like this," said Rachel: "it's very like Jamaica."

"This isn't England," said John, "you stupid!"

"But it must be," said Rachel: "England's where we're going."

"We don't get to England yet," said John: "it must be somewhere we're stopping at, like when we got all those turtles."

"I like stopping at places," said Laura.

"I don't," said Rachel.

"I do, though," pursued Laura.

"Where are those young men gone?" Margaret asked the mate. "Are they coming back?"

"They'll just come back to be paid, after we've sold the cargo," he answered.

"Then they're not living on the ship?" she pursued.

"No, we hired them from Havana."

"But what for?"

He looked at her in surprise: "Why, those are the 'ladies' we had on board, to look like passengers—You didn't think they were real ladies, did you?"

"What, were they dressed up?" asked Emily excitedly: "What fun!"

"I like dressing up," said Laura.

"I don't," said Rachel, "I think it's babyish."

"*I* thought they were real ladies," admitted Emily.

"We're a respectable ship's crew, we are," said the mate, a trifle stiffly—and without too good logic, when you come to think of it. "Here, you go on shore and amuse yourselves."

So the children went ashore, holding hands in a long row, and promenaded the town in a formal sort of way. Laura wanted to go off by herself, but the others would not let her: and when they returned, the line was still unbroken. They had seen all there was to see, and no one had taken the least notice of them (so far as they were aware), and they wanted to start asking questions again.

It was, then, a charming little sleepy old place, in its way, this Santa Lucia: isolated on the forgotten western end of Cuba between Nombre de Dios and the Rio de Puercos: cut off from the open sea by the intricate nature of the channels through the reefs and the Banks of Isabella, channels only navigable to the practiced and creeping local coasting craft and shunned like poison by bigger traffic: on land isolated by a hundred miles of forest from Havana.

Time was, these little ports of the Canal de Guaniguanico had been pretty prosperous, as bases for pirates: but it was a fleeting prosperity. There came the heroic attack of an American squadron under Captain Allen, in 1823, on the Bay of Sejuapo, their headquarters. From that blow (although it took many years to take full effect) the industry never really recovered: it dwindled and dwindled, like hand-weaving. One could make money much faster in a city like Havana, and with less risk (if less respectably). Piracy had long since ceased to pay, and should have been scrapped years ago: but a vocational tradition will last on a long time after it has ceased to be economic, in a decadent form. Now, Santa Lucia—and piracy—continued to exist because they always had: but for no other reason. Such a haul as the *Clorinda* did not come once in a blue moon. Every year the amount of land under cultivation dwindled, and the pirate schooners were abandoned to rot against the wharves or ignominiously sold as traders. The young men left for Havana or the United States. The maidens yawned. The local grandees increased in dignity as their numbers and property dwindled: an idyllic, simple-minded country community, oblivious of the outer world and of its own approaching oblivion.

"I don't think I should like to live here," John decided, when they got back to the ship.

Meanwhile the cargo had been unloaded onto the quay: and after the siesta a crowd of about a hundred people gathered round, poking and discussing. The auction was about to begin. Captain Jonsen tramped about rather in the way of everybody, but especially annoying the mate by shouting contrary directions every minute. The latter had a ledger, and a number of labels with numbers on them which he was pasting onto the various bales and packages. The sailors were building a kind of temporary stage—the thing was to be done in style.

Every moment the crowd increased. Because they all talked Spanish it was a pantomime to the children: like puppets acting, not like real people moving and talking. So they discovered what a fascinating game it is to watch foreigners, whose very simplest words mean nothing to you, and try to guess what they are about.

Moreover, these were all such funny-looking people: they moved about as if they were kings, and spat all the time, and smoked thin black cigars, the blue smoke of which ascended from their enormous hats as from censers.

At one moment there was a diversion—the crowd suddenly gaped, and there staggered onto the stage the whole crew of the schooner carrying a huge pair of scales: it was always on the point of being too much for them, and running suddenly away with them in another direction.

There were quite a number of ladies in the crowd—old ones, they seemed to the children. Some were thin and dried up, like monkeys: but most were fat, and one was fatter than all of them and treated with the greatest respect (perhaps for her mustache). She was the wife of the Chief Magistrate—Señora del Illustrious Juzgado del Municipal de Santa Lucia, to give her her title. She had a rocking-chair of suitable strength and width, which was carried by a short squinting negro and set in the very middle of the scene, right in front of the platform. There she throned herself: and the negro stood behind her, holding a violet silk sunshade over her head.

No one can doubt that she immediately became the most noticeable thing in the picture.

She had a powerful bass voice, and when she uttered some jocundity (as she repeatedly did), every one heard it, however much they were chattering among themselves.

The children, as was their custom, wormed their way without any excess of civility through the crowd and grouped themselves round her throne.

The captain either did not know, or suddenly refused to know, a single word of Spanish: so the auctioneering devolved on the mate. The latter mounted the stage: and with a great assumption of competence began.

But auctioneering is an art: it is as easy to write a sonnet in a foreign tongue as to conduct a successful auction. One must have at one's command eloquence without a hitch: the faculty of kindling an audience, amusing them, castigating them, converting them, till they rattle out increments as a camp-meeting rattles out Amens: till they totally forget the worth (and even the nature) of the lot, and begin to take a real pride in a long run of bidding—as a champion does in a long break at billiards.

This little Viennese had been to a good school, it is true: for he had once resided in Wales, where one sees auctioneering in its finest flower. In Welsh, or English, or even in his native tongue, he could have acquitted himself fairly well: but in Spanish, just that margin of power was lacking to him. The audience remained stern, cold, critical, bidding grudgingly.

As if this language difficulty were not in itself enough, there sat that overpowering old dame on her throne, distracting with her jokes whatever vestige of attention he might otherwise have managed to arouse.

When the third lot of coffee came to be dealt with, there was even the beginning of a rather nasty row. The children were highly scandalized: they had never seen grown-ups being rude to one another before. The captain had undertaken the weighing: and it was something to do with a habit he had of leaning against the scales while he read them. Being short-sighted, he could see the figures much more clearly like that: but it displeased the buyers, and they had a lot to say about it.

The captain, mortified, wrung his hands, and began to answer them in Danish. They rejoined in Spanish even more stingingly. He stumped off in a sulk: they could all conduct his affairs without him, if they weren't prepared to treat him with a little consideration.

But who would be less partial? The mate, angry,

maintained that to elect one of the buyers was equally objectionable.

Thereon an earthquake began in the fat old lady, and gradually gathered enough force to lift her onto her feet. She took John by the shoulders, and pushed him before her to the scales. Then in a few witty, ringing words she suggested her solution—*he* should do the weighing.

The audience were pleased: but as soon as John understood he went very red, and wanted to escape. The rest of the children, on the other hand, were eaten with envy.

"Mayn't I help too?" piped Rachel.

The despairing mate thought he saw just a forlorn hope in this. While John was being instructed, he gathered the other children: and out of the heap of miscellaneous clothing rigged them all out in a sort of fancy dress. Then he gave them the samples to carry round, and the sale began anew.

It had now assumed rather the character of a parochial bazaar. Even the Vicar was present—though less well shaved than he would have been in England, and cunninger-looking. He was one of the only buyers.

The children thoroughly enjoyed themselves, and minced and pranced and tugged each other's turbans. But the crowd was a Latin one, not Nordic: and their endearing tricks failed altogether to arouse any interest. The sale went worse than ever.

There was only one exception, and that was the important old lady. Once her attention had been called (by her own act) to the children, it fixed itself on one of them, on Edward. She drew him to her bosom, like a mother in melodrama, and with her hairy mouth gave him three resounding kisses.

Edward could no more have struggled than if caught by a boa. Moreover, the portentous woman fascinated him, as if she had been a boa indeed. He lay in her arms limp, self-conscious, and dejected: but without active thought of escape.

And so the business went on: on the one hand the unheeded drone of the mate, on the other the great creature still keeping up her witticisms, still dominating everything: all of a sudden remembering Edward, and giving him a couple of kisses like so many bombs: then clean forgetting all about him: then remembering him again, and hugging him: then dropping her salts: then nearly dropping Edward: then suddenly twisting round to launch a dart into the crowd behind her—she was the despair of that unhappy auctioneer, who saw lot after lot fall for a tenth of its value, or even find no bidder at all.

Captain Jonsen, however, had his own idea of how to enliven a parochial bazaar that is proving a frost. He went on board, and mixed several gallons of that potion known in alcoholic circles as Hangman's Blood (which is compounded of rum, gin, brandy, and porter). Innocent (merely beery) as it looks, refreshing as it tastes, it has the property of increasing rather than allaying thirst, and so, once it has made a breach, soon demolishes the whole fort.

This he poured out into mugs, merely remarking that it was a noted English cordial, and gave it to the children to distribute among the crowd.

At once the Cubans began to show more interest in them than when they came bearing samples of arrowroot: and with their popularity their happiness increased, and like rococo Ganymedekins and Hebelettes they darted about the crowd, distributing the enticing poison to all who would.

When he saw what was on foot, the mate wiped his mouth in despair.

"*Oh* you fool!" he groaned.

But the captain himself was highly pleased with his ruse: kept rubbing his hands, and grinning, and winking.

"That'll liven 'em, eh?"

"Wait and see!" was all the mate let himself say. "You just wait and see!"

"Look at Edward!" said Emily to Margaret in a pause. "It's perfectly sickening!"

It was. The very first mug rendered the fat señora even more motherly. Edward by now was fascinated, was in her power completely. He sat and gazed up in her little black eyes, his own large brown ones glazed with sentiment. He avoided her mustache, it is true: but on her cheek he was returning her kisses earnestly. All this, of course, without the possibility of their exchanging a single word— pure instinct. "With a fork drive Nature out . . ." one would gladly have taken a fork to Nature, on that occasion.

Meanwhile, on the rest of the crowd the liquor was having exactly the effect the mate had foreseen. Instead of stimulating them, it dissolved completely whatever vestiges of attention they were still giving to the sale. He stepped down from the platform—gave it all up in despair. For they had now broken up into little groups, which discussed and argued their own affairs as if they were in a café. He in his turn went on board, and shut himself in his cabin—Captain Jonsen could deal with the mess he had made himself!

But alas! No worse host than Jonsen was ever born: he was utterly incapable of either understanding or controlling a crowd. All he could think of doing was plying them with more.

For the children the spectacle was an absorbing one. The whole nature of these people, as they drank, seemed to be changing: under their very eyes something seemed to be breaking up, like ice melting. Remember that to them this was a pantomime: no word spoken to explain, and so the eyes exercised a peculiar clearness.

It was rather as if the whole crowd had been immersed in water, and something dissolved out of them while the general structure yet remained. The tone of their voices changed, and they began to talk much slower, to move more slowly and elaborately. The expression of their faces became more candid, and yet more mask-like: hiding less, there was also less to hide. Two men even began to fight: but they fought so incompetently it was like a fight in a poetic play. Conversation, which before had a beginning and an end, now grew shapeless and interminable, and the women laughed a lot.

One old gentleman in most respectable clothes settled himself on the dirty ground at full length, with his head in the shade of the throned lady, spread a handkerchief over his face, and went to sleep: three other middle-aged men, holding each other with one hand to establish contact and using the other for emphasis, kept up a continuous clacking talk, that faltered intolerably though never quite stopping—like a very old engine.

A dog ran in and out among them all wagging its tail, but no one kicked it. Presently it found the old gentleman who was asleep on the ground, and began licking his ear excitedly: it had never had such a chance before.

The old lady also had fallen asleep, a little crookedly— she might even have slipped off her chair if her negro had not buttressed her up. Edward got off her, and went and joined the other children rather shamefacedly: but they would not speak to him.

Jonsen looked round him perplexedly. Why had Otto abandoned the sale, now the crowd were all primed and ready? Probably he had some good reason, though. He was an incomprehensible man, that mate: but clever.

The truth is that Captain Jonsen was himself a man with a very weak head for liquor, and so he very seldom touched it, and knew little of the subtler aspects of its effects.

He paced up and down the dusty wharf at his usual slow shuffle, his head sunk forward in wretchedness, occasionally wringing his hands in the naturalest way, and even whimpering. When the priest came up to him confidentially and offered him a price for all that remained unsold he simply shook his head and continued his shuffle.

THERE WAS SOMETHING a little nightmare-like in the whole scene which riveted the children's attention, and was very near the border of frightening them. It was with something of a struggle that at last Margaret said "Let's go on the ship." So they all went on board: and feeling a little unprotected even there, descended into the hold, which was the safest place because they had already slept in it. They sat down on the kelson without doing or saying much, still with a vague apprehension, till boredom at last eliminated it.

"Oh I *wish* I had brought my paint-box!" said Emily, with a sigh fetched right up from her boots.

II

That night, after they had all gone to bed, they saw in a half-asleep state a lantern bobbing up and down in the open hatch. It was held by José, the little monkeyfied one (they had already decided he was the nicest of the crew). He was grinning winningly, and beckoning to them.

Emily was too sleepy to move, and so were Laura and Rachel: so leaving them to lie, the others—Margaret, Edward, and John—scrambled on deck.

It was mysteriously quiet. Not a sign of the crew, but for José. In the bright starlight the town looked unnormally beautiful: there was music coming from one of the big houses up by the church. José conducted them ashore and up to this house: tiptoed up to the jalousies and signed to them to follow him.

As the light struck his face it became transfigured, so affected was he by the opulence within.

The children craned up to the level of the windows and peered in too, oblivious of the mosquitoes making havoc of their necks.

It was a very grand sight. This was the house of the Chief Magistrate: and he was giving a dinner in honor of Captain Jonsen and his mate. There he sat at the head of the table, in uniform; very stiff, yet his little beard even stiffer than himself. His was the kind of dignity that grows from reserve and stillness, from freezing every minute like game which scents the hunter: while in total contrast to him there sat his wife (the important señora who had made so much of Edward), far more impressive than her husband, but doing it not by dignity but by that calculated abandon and vulgarity which transcends dignity. Indeed, her flinging about got the greater part of its effect from the very formality of her setting.

When the children arrived at the window she must even have been discussing the size of her own belly: for she suddenly seized the shy hand of the mate, and made him, willy-nilly, feel it, as if to clench an argument.

As for her husband, he did not seem to see her: nor did the servants: she was such a very great lady.

But it was not her, it was the meal which raped José's attention. It was certainly an impressive one. Together on the table were tomato soup, mountain mullet, cray-fish, a huge red-snapper, land-crabs, rice and fried chicken, a young turkey, a small joint of goat-mutton, a wild duck, beef steak, fried pork, a dish of wild pigeons, sweet potatoes, yuca, wine, and guavas and cream.

It was a meal which would take a long time.

Captain Jonsen and the lady appeared to be on excellent terms: he pressing some project on her, and she, without the least loss of amiability, putting it on one side. What they were talking about, of course, the children could not hear. As a matter of fact, it was themselves. Captain Jonsen was trying to get the lady to discuss the disposal of his impromptu nursery: the most reasonable solution being plainly to leave them at Santa Lucia, more or less in her charge. But she was adept at eluding the importunate. It was not till the banquet was over that he realized he had failed to make any arrangement whatever.

But long before this, before the dinner was ended and the dance began, the children were tired of the peep-show. So José tiptoed away with them, down to the back streets by the dock. Presently they came to a mysterious door at the bottom of a staircase, with a negro standing as if on guard. But he made no effort to stop them, and, José leading them, they climbed several flights to a large upper room.

The air was one you could hardly push through. The place was crowded with negroes, and a few rather smudgy whites: among whom they recognized most of the rest of the crew of the schooner. At the far end was the most primitive stage you ever saw: there was a cradle on it, and a large star swung on the end of a piece of string. There was to be a nativity-play—rather early in the season. While the Chief Magistrate entertained the pirate captain and mate, the priest had got this up in honor of the pirate crew.

A nativity play, with real cattle.

The whole audience had arrived an hour early, so as to see the entry of the cow. The children were just in time for this.

The room was in the upper part of a warehouse, which had been built, through some freak of vanity, in the English fashion, several stories high; and was provided with the usual large door opening onto nothingness, with a beam-and-tackle over it. Many the load of gold-dust and arrowroot which must have once been hoisted into it: now, like most of the others at Santa Lucia, it had long since ceased to be used.

But to-day a new rope had been rove through the block: and a broad belly-band put round the waist of the priest's protesting old cow.

Margaret and Edward lingered timidly near the top of the stairs; but John, putting his head down and burrowing like a mole, was not content till he had reached the open doorway. There he stood looking out into the darkness: where he saw a slowly revolving cow treading the air a yard from the sill, while at each revolution a negro reached out to the utmost limit of balance, trying to catch her by the tail and draw her to shore.

John, in his excitement, leaned out too far. He lost his balance and fell clear to the ground, forty feet, right on his head.

José gave a cry of alarm, sprang onto the cow's back, and was instantly lowered away—just as if the cinema had already been invented. He must have looked very comic. But what was going on inside him the while it is difficult to know. Such a responsibility does not often fall on an old sailor; and he would probably feel it all the more for that reason. As for the crowd beneath, they made no attempt to touch the body till José had completed his descent: they stood back and let him have a good look at it, and shake it, and so on. But the neck was quite plainly broken.

Margaret and Edward, however, had not any clear idea of what was going on, since they had not actually seen John fall. So they were rather annoyed when two of the schooner's crew appeared and insisted on their coming back to bed at once. They wanted to know where John was: but even more they wanted to know where José was, and why they weren't to be allowed to stay. However they obeyed, in the impossibility of asking questions, and started back to bed.

Just as they were about to go on board the schooner, they heard a huge report on their left, like a cannon. They turned; and looking past the quiet, silver town, with its palm-groves, to the hills behind, they saw a large ball of fire, traveling at a tremendous rate. It was quite close to the ground: and not very far off either—just beyond the Church. It left a wake of the most brilliant blue, green, and purple blobs of light. For a while it hovered: then it burst, and the air was shortly charged with a strong sulphurous smell.

They were all frightened, the sailors even more than the children, and hastened on board.

IN THE SMALL hours, Edward suddenly called Emily in his sleep. She woke up: "What is it?"

"It's rather cow-catching, isn't it?" he asked anxiously, his eyes tight shut.

"What's the matter?"

He did not answer, so she roused him—or thought she had.

"I only wanted to see if you were a *real* Cow-catching Zomfanelia," he explained in a kind voice: and was immediately deep asleep again.

In the morning they might easily have thought the whole thing a dream—if John's bed had not been so puzzlingly empty.

Yet, as if by some mute flash of understanding, no one

commented on his absence. No one questioned Margaret, and she offered no information. Neither then nor thereafter was his name ever mentioned by anybody: and if you had known the children intimately you would never have guessed from *them* that he had ever existed.

III

The children's only enemy on board the schooner (which presently put to sea again, with them still on board) was the big white pig. (There was a little black fellow, too.)

He was a pig with no decision of mind. He could never choose a place to lie for himself; but was so ready to follow any one else's opinion, that whatever position you took up he immediately recognized as the best, the only site: and came and routed you out of it. Seeing how rare shady patches of deck are in a calm, or dry patches in a stiff breeze, this was a most infernal nuisance. One is so defenseless against big pigs when lying on one's back.

The little black one could be a nuisance also, it is true—but that was only from excess of friendliness. He hated to be left out of any party: nay more, he hated lying on inanimate matter if a living couch was to be found.

On the north beach of Cape San Antonio it is possible to land a boat, if you pick your spot. About fifty yards through the bushes there are a couple of acres of open ground: cross this, and among some sharp coral rocks in the scrub on the far side are two wells, the northernmost the better of the two.

So, being becalmed off the Mangrove Keys one morning, Jonsen sent a boat on shore to get water.

The heat was extreme. The ropes hung like dead snakes, the sails as heavy as ill-sculptured drapery. The iron stanchion of the awning blistered any hand that touched it. Where the deck was unsheltered, the pitch boiled out of the seams. The children lay gasping together in the small shade, the little black pig squealing anxiously till he found a comfortable stomach to settle down on.

The big white pig had not found them yet.

From the silent shore came an occasional gunshot. The water-party were potting pigeons. The sea was like a smooth pampas of quicksilver: so steady you could not split shore from reflection, till the casual collision of a pelican broke the phantom. The crew were mending sails, under the awning, with infinite slowness: all except one negro, who straddled the bowsprit in his trousers, admiring his own grin in the mirror beneath. The sun lit an iridescent glimmer on his shoulders: in such a light even a negro could not be black.

Emily was missing John badly: but the little black pig

snuffled in supreme content, his snout buried amicably in her armpit.

When the boatload returned, they had other game besides pigeons and gray land-crabs. They had stolen a goat from some lonely fisherman.

It was just as they came up over the side that the big white pig discovered the party under the awning, and prepared for the attack. But the goat at that moment bounded nimbly from the bulwarks: and without even stopping to look round, swallowed his chin and charged. He caught the old pig full in the ribs, knocking his wind out completely.

Then the battle began. The goat charged, the pig screamed and hustled. Each time the goat arrived at him the pig yelled as if he was killed; but each time the goat drew back the pig advanced towards him. The goat, his beard flying like a prophet's, his eyes crimson and his scut as lively as a lamb's at the teat, bounded in, bounded back into the bows for a fresh run: but at each charge his run grew shorter and shorter. The pig was hemming him in.

Suddenly the pig gave a frightful squeal, chiefly in surprise at his own temerity, and pounced. He had got the goat cornered against the windlass: and for a few flashing seconds bit and trampled.

It was a very chastened goat which was presently led off to his quarters: but the children were prepared to love him for ever, for the heroic bangs he had given the old tyrant.

BUT HE WAS not entirely inhuman, that pig. That same afternoon, he was lying on the hatch eating a banana. The ship's monkey was swinging on a loose tail of rope; and spotting the prize, swung further and further till at last he was able to snatch it from between his very trotters. You would never have thought that the immobile mask of a pig could wear a look of such astonishment, such dismay, such piteous injury.

5

WHEN DESTINY KNOCKS the first nail in the coffin of a tyrant, it is seldom long before she knocks the last.

It was the very next morning that the schooner, in the lightest of airs, was sidling gently to leeward. The mate was at the wheel, shifting his weight from foot to foot with that rhythmic motion many steersmen affect, the better to get the feel of a finicky helm; and Edward was teaching the captain's terrier to beg, on the cabin-top. The mate shouted to him to hang on to something.

"Why?" said Edward.

"*Hang on!*" cried the mate again, spinning the wheel over as fast as he could to bring her into the wind.

The howling squall took her, through his promptness, almost straight in the nose; or it would have carried all away. Edward clung to the skylight. The terrier skidded about alarmedly all over the cabin-top, slipped off onto the deck, and was kicked by a dashing sailor clean through the galley door. But not so that poor big pig, who was taking an airing on deck at the time. Overboard he went, and vanished to windward, his snout (sometimes) sticking up manfully out of the water. God, Who had sent him the goat and the monkey for a sign, now required his soul of him. Overboard, too, went the coops of fowls, three new-washed shirts, and—of all strange things to get washed away—the grind-stone.

Up out of his cabin appeared the captain's shapeless brown head, cursing the mate as if it was *he* who had upset the apple-cart. He came up without his boots, in gray wool socks, and his braces hanging down his back.

"Get below!" muttered the mate furiously. "I can manage her!"

The captain did not, however: still in his socks, he came up on deck and took the wheel out of the mate's hand. The latter went a dull brick-red: walked for'ard: then aft again: then went below and shut himself in his cabin.

In a few moments the wind had combed up some quite hearty waves: then it blew their tops off, and so flattened the sea out again, a sea that was black except for little whipt-up fountains of iridescent foam.

"Get my boots!" bellowed Jonsen at Edward.

Edward dashed down the companion with alacrity. It is a great moment, one's first order at sea; especially when it comes in an emergency. He reappeared with a boot in each hand, and a lurch flung him boots and all at the captain's feet. "Never carry things in both hands," said the captain, smiling pleasantly.

"Why?" asked Edward.

"Keep one hand to lay hold with."

There was a pause.

"Some day I will teach you the three Sovereign Rules of Life." He shook his head meditatively. "They are very wise. But not yet. You are too young."

"Why not?" asked Edward. "When shall I be old enough?"

The captain considered, going over the Rules in his head.

"When you know which is windward and which is lee-ward, then I will teach you the first rule."

Edward made his way forward, determined to qualify as soon as he possibly could.

When the worst of the squall was over they got the ad-vantage of it, the schooner lying over lissomly and spin-ning along like a race-horse. The crew were in great spirits—chaffing the carpenter, who, they declared, had thrown his grind-stone overboard as a lifebuoy for the pig.

The children were in good spirits also. Their shyness was all gone now. The schooner lying over as she did, her wet deck made a most admirable toboggan-slide; and for half an hour they tobogganed happily on their bottoms from windward to leeward, shrieking with joy, fetching up in the lee-scuppers, which were mostly awash, and then climbing from thing to thing to the windward bulwarks raised high in the air, and so all over again.

Throughout that half hour, Jonsen at the wheel said not a single word. But at last his pent-up irritation broke out:

"Hi! You! Stop that!"

They gazed at him in astonishment and disillusion.

There is a period in the relations of children with any new grown-up in charge of them, the period between first acquaintance and the first reproof, which can only be compared to the primordial innocence of Eden. Once a reproof has been administered, this can never be recovered again.

Jonsen now had done it.

But he was not content with that—he was still bursting with rage:

"Stop it! Stop it, I tell you!"

(They had already done so, of course.)

The whole unreasonableness, the monstrousness of the imposition of these brats on his ship suddenly came over him, and summed itself up in a single symbol:

"If you go and wear holes in your drawers, do you think *I* am going to mend them?—Lieber Gott! What do you think I am, eh? What do you think this ship is? What do you think we all are? To mend your drawers for you, eh? *To mend . . . your . . . drawers!*"

There was a pause, while they all stood thunderstruck. But even now he had not finished:

"Where do you think you'll get new ones, eh?" he asked, in a voice explosive with rage. Then he added, with an insulting coarseness of tone: "And I'll not have you going about my ship without them! See?"

Scarlet to the eyes with outrage they retreated to the bows. They could hardly believe so unspeakable a remark had crossed human lips. They assumed an air of lightness, and talked together in studied loud voices: but their joy was dashed for the day.

So it was that—small as a man's hand—a specter began to show over their horizon: the suspicion at last that this was *not* all according to plan, that they might even not be wanted. For a while their actions showed the unhappy wariness of the uninvited guest.

Later in the afternoon, Jonsen, who had not spoken again, but looked from time to time acutely miserable, was still at the wheel. The mate had shaved himself and put on shore clothes, as a parable: he now appeared on deck: pretended not to see the captain, but strolled like a passenger up to the children and entered into conversation with them.

"If I'm not fit to steer in foul weather, I'm not fit to steer in fair!" he muttered, but without glancing at the captain. "He can take the helm all day and night, for all the help *I'll* give him!"

The captain appeared equally not to see the mate. He looked quite ready to take both watches till kingdom come.

"If *he'd* been at the wheel when that squall struck us," said the mate under his voice but with biting passion, "he'd have lost the ship! He's no more eye for a squall coming than a sucker-fish! And he knows it, too: that's what makes him go on this way!"

The children did not answer. It shocked them deeply to have to see a grown-up, a should-be Olympian, displaying his feelings. In exact opposition to the witnesses at the Transfiguration, they felt it would have been good for them to be almost anywhere rather than there. He was totally unconscious of their discomfort, however: too self-occupied to notice how they avoided catching his eye.

"Look! There's a steamship!" exclaimed Margaret, with much too bright a brightness.

The mate glowered at it.

"Aye, they'll be the death of us, those steamers," he said. "Every year there's more of them. They'll be using them for men-of-war next, and then where'll we be? Times are bad enough without steamers."

But while he spoke he wore a preoccupied expression, as if he were more concerned with what was going on at the back of his mind than with what went on in the front.

"Did you ever hear about what happened when the first steamer put to sea in the Gulf of Paria?" he asked, however.

"No, what?" asked Margaret, with an eagerness that even exceeded the necessities of politeness in its falsity.

"She was built on the Clyde, and sailed over. (Nobody thought of using steam for a long ocean voyage in those days.) The Company thought they ought to make a to-do—to popularize her, so to speak. So the first time she put to sea under her own power, they invited all the big-wigs on board: all the Members of Assembly in Trinidad, and the Governor and his Staff, and a Bishop. It was the Bishop what did the trick."

His story died out: he became completely absorbed in watching sidelong the effect of his bravado on the captain.

"Did what?" asked Margaret.

"Ran 'em aground."

"But what did they let him steer for?" asked Edward. "They might have known he couldn't!"

"Edward! How dare you talk about a Bishop in that rude way!" admonished Rachel.

"It wasn't the steamer he ran aground, sonny," said the mate: "it was a poor innocent little devil of a pirate craft, that was just beating up for the Boca Grande in a northerly breeze."

"Good for him!" said Edward. "How did he do it?"

"They were all sea-sick, being on a steamer for the first time: the way she rolls, not like a decent sailing-vessel. There wasn't a man who could stay on deck—except the Bishop, and he just thrived on it. So when the poor little pirate cut under her bows, and seen her coming up in the eye of the wind, no sail set, with a cloud of smoke amidships and an old Bishop bung in the middle of the smoke, and her paddles making as much turmoil as a whale trying to scratch a flea in its ear, he just beached his vessel and took to the woods. Never went to sea again, he didn't; started growing cocoa-nuts. But there was one poor fish was in such a hurry he broke his leg, and they came ashore and found him. When he saw the Bishop coming for him he started yelling out it was the Devil."

"O-oh!" gasped Rachel, horror-struck.

"How silly of him," said Edward.

"I don't know so much!" said the mate. "He wasn't too far wrong! Ever since that, they've been the death of our profession, Steam and the Church . . . what with steaming, and what with preaching, and steaming and preaching. . . . Now that's a funny thing," he broke off, suddenly interested by what he was saying: "*Steam* and the *Church*! What have they got in common, eh? Nothing, you'd say: you'd think they'd fight each other cat-and-dog: but no: they're thick as two thieves ... thick as thieves.—Not like in the days of Parson Audain."

"Who was he?" asked Margaret helpfully.

"He was a right sort of a parson, he was, *yn wyr iawn*! He was Rector of Roseau—oh, a long time back."

"Here! Come and take this wheel while I have a spell!" grunted the captain.

"I couldn't well say *how* long back," continued the mate in a loud, unnatural, and now slightly exultant voice: "forty years or more."

He began to tell the story of the famous Rector of Roseau: one of the finest pathetic preachers of his age, according to contemporaries; whose appearance was fine, gentle, and venerable, and who supplemented his stipend by owning a small privateer.

"Here! Otto!" called Jonsen.

But the mate had a long recital of the parson's misfortunes before him: beginning with the capture of his schooner (while smuggling negroes to Guadaloupe) by another privateer, from Nevis; and how the parson went to Nevis, posted his rival's name on the court-house door, and stood on guard there with loaded pistols for three days in the hope the man would come and challenge him.

"What, to fight a *duel*?" asked Harry.

"But wasn't he a clergyman, you said?" asked Emily.

But duels, it appeared, did not come amiss to this priest. He fought thirteen altogether in his life, the mate told them: and on one occasion, while waiting for the seconds to reload, he went up to his opponent, suggested "just a little something to fill in time, good sir"—and knocked him flat with his fist.

This time, however, his enemy lay low: so he fitted out a second schooner, and took command of her, week-days, himself. His first quarry was an apparently harmless Spanish merchantman: but she suddenly opened fourteen masked gun-ports and it was he who had to surrender. All his crew were massacred but himself and his carpenter, who hid behind a water-cask all night.

"But I don't understand," said Margaret: "was he a pirate?"

"Of course he was!" said Otto the mate.

"Then *why* did you say he was a clergyman?" pursued Emily.

The mate looked as puzzled as she did. "Well, he was Rector of Roseau, wasn't he? And B.A., B.D.? Anyway, he was Rector until the new Governor listened to some cock-and-bull story against him, and made him resign. He was the best preacher they ever had—he'd have been a Bishop one day, if some one hadn't slandered him to the Governor!"

"Otto!" called the captain in a conciliatory voice. "Come over here, I want to speak to you."

But the deaf and exulting mate had plenty of his story still to run: how Audain now turned trader, and took a cargo of corn to San Domingo, and settled there: how he challenged two black generals to a duel, and shot them both, and Christophe threatened to hang him if they died. But the parson (having little faith in Domingan doctors) escaped by night in an open boat and went to St. Eustatius. There he found many religions but no ministers; so he recommended clergyman of every kind: in the morning he celebrated a mass for the Catholics, then a Lutheran service in Dutch, then Church of England matins: in the evening he sang hymns and preached hell-fire to the Methodists. Meanwhile his wife, who had more tranquil tastes, lived at Bristol: so he now married a Dutch widow, resourcefully conducting the ceremony himself.

"But I *don't* understand!" said Emily despairingly: "Was he a real clergyman?"

"Of course he wasn't," said Margaret.

"But he couldn't have married himself *himself* if he wasn't," argued Edward. "Could he?"

The mate heaved a sigh.

"But the English Church aren't like that nowadays," he said. "They're all against us."

"I should think not, indeed!" pronounced Rachel slowly, in a deep indignant voice. "He was a very wicked man!"

"He was a most respectable person," replied the mate severely, "and a *wonderful* pathetic preacher!—You may take it they were chagrined at Roseau, when they heard St. Eustatius had got him!"

Captain Jonsen had lashed the wheel, and came up, his face piteous with distress.

"Otto! Mein Schatz...!" he began, laying his great bear's-arm round the mate's neck. Without more ado they went below together, and a sailor came aft unbidden and took the wheel.

TEN MINUTES LATER the mate reappeared on deck for a moment, and sought out the children.

"What's the captain been saying to you?" he asked. "Flashed out at you about something, did he?"

He took their complex, uncomfortable silence for assent.

"Don't you take too much notice of what he says," he went on. "He flashes out like that sometimes; but a minute after he could eat himself, fair eat himself!"

The children stared at him in astonishment: what on earth was he trying to say?

But he seemed to think he had explained his mission fully: turned, and once more went below.

FOR HOURS A merry but rather tedious hubble-bubble, suggesting liquor, was heard ascending from the cabin skylight. As evening drew on, the breeze having dropped away almost to a calm, the steersman reported that both Jonsen and Otto were now fast asleep, their heads on each other's shoulders across the cabin table. As he had long forgotten what the course was, but had been simply steering by the wind, and there was now no wind to steer by, he (the steersman) concluded the wheel could get on very well without him.

The reconciliation of the captain and the mate deserved to be celebrated by all hands with a blind.

A rum-cask was broached: and the common sailors were soon as unconscious as their betters.

Altogether this was one of the unpleasantest days the children had spent in their lives.

When dawn came, every one was still pretty incapable, and the neglected vessel drooped uncertainly. Jonsen, still rather unsteady on his feet, his head aching and his mind Napoleonic but muddled, came on deck and looked about him. The sun had come up like a searchlight: but it was about all there was to be seen. No land was anywhere in sight, and the sea and sky seemed very uncertain as to the most becoming place to locate their mutual firmament. It was not till he had looked round and round a fair number of times that he perceived a vessel, up in what by all appearances must be sky, yet not very far distant.

For some little while he could not remember what it is a pirate captain does when he sees a sail; and he felt in no mood to overtax his brain by trying to. But after a time it came back unbidden—one gives chase.

"Give chase!" he ordered solemnly to the morning air: and then went below again and roused the mate, who roused the crew.

No one had the least idea where they were, or what kind of a craft this quarry might be: but such considerations were altogether too complicated for the moment. As the sun parted further from his reflection a breeze sprang up: so the sails were trimmed after a fashion, and chase was duly given.

In an hour or two, as the air grew clearer, it was plain their quarry was a merchant brig, not too heavily laden, and making a fair pace: a pace, indeed, which in their incompetently trimmed condition they were finding it pretty difficult to equal. Jonsen shuffled rapidly up and down the deck like a shuttle, passing his woof backwards and forwards through the real business of the ship. He was hugging himself with excitement, trying to evolve some crafty scheme of capture. The chase went on: but noon passed, the distance between the two vessels was barely, if at all, lessened. Jonsen, however, was much too optimistic to realize this.

It used to be a common device of pirates when in chase of a vessel to tow behind them a spare topmast, or some other bulky object. This would act as a drogue, or brake: and the pursued, seeing them with all sail set apparently doing their utmost, would under-estimate their powers of speed. Then when night fell the pirate would haul the spar on board, overtake the other vessel rapidly, and catch it unprepared.

There were several reasons why this device was unsuitable to the present occasion. First and most obviously, it was doubtful whether, in their present condition, they were capable of overtaking the brig at all, leaving such handicaps altogether out of consideration. A second was that the brig showed no signs of alarm. She was proceeding on her voyage at her natural pace, quite unaware of the honor they were doing her.

However, Captain Jonsen was nothing if not a crafty man; and during the afternoon he gave orders for a spare spar to be towed behind as I have described. The result was that the schooner lost ground rapidly: and when night fell they were at least a couple of miles further from the brig than they had been at dawn. When night fell, of course, they hauled the spar on board and prepared for the last act. They followed the brig by compass through the hours of darkness, without catching sight of her. When morning came, all hands crowded expectantly at the rail.

But the brig was vanished. The sea was as bare as an egg.

If they were lost before, now they were double-lost. Jonsen did not know where he might be within two hundred miles; and being no sextant-man, but an incurable dead-reckoner, he had no means of finding out. This did not worry him very greatly, however, because sooner or later one of two things might happen: he might catch sight of some bit of land he recognized, or he might capture some vessel better informed than himself. Meanwhile, since he had no particular destination, one bit of sea was much the same to him as another.

The piece he was wandering in, however, was evidently out of the main track of shipping; for days went by, and weeks, without his coming even so near to effecting a capture as he had been in the case of the brig.

But Captain Jonsen was not sorry to be out of the public eye for a while. Before he had left Santa Lucia, news had reached him of the *Clorinda* putting into Havana; and of the fantastic tale Marpole was telling. The "twelve masked gun-ports" had amused him hugely, since he was altogether without artillery: but when he heard Marpole accused him of murdering the children—Marpole, that least reputable of skunks—his anger had broken out in one of its sudden explosions. For it was unthinkable—during those first few days—that he would ever touch a hair of their heads, or even speak a cross word to them. They were still a sort of holy novelty then: it was not till their shyness had worn off that he had begun to regret so whole-heartedly the failure of his attempt to leave them behind with the Chief Magistrate's wife.

6

THE WEEKS PASSED in aimless wandering. For the
children, the lapse of time acquired once more the tex-
ture of a dream: things ceased happening: every inch of
the schooner was now as familiar to them as the *Clorinda*
had been, or Ferndale: they settled down quietly to grow,
as they had done at Ferndale, and as they would have
done, had there been time, on the *Clorinda*.

And then an event did occur, to Emily, of considerable
importance. She suddenly realized who she was.

There is little reason that one can see why it should not
have happened to her five years earlier, or even five later;
and none, why it should have come that particular afternoon.

She had been playing houses in a nook right in the
bows, behind the windlass (on which she had hung a

devil's-claw as a door-knocker); and tiring of it was walking rather aimlessly aft, thinking vaguely about some bees and a fairy queen, when it suddenly flashed into her mind that she was *she*.

She stopped dead, and began looking over all of her person which came within the range of eyes. She could not see much, except a fore-shortened view of the front of her frock, and her hands when she lifted them for inspection: but it was enough for her to form a rough idea of the little body she suddenly realized to be hers.

She began to laugh, rather mockingly. "Well!" she thought, in effect: "Fancy *you*, of all people, going and getting caught like this!—You can't get out of it now, not for a very long time: you'll have to go through with being a child, and growing up, and getting old, before you'll be quit of this mad prank!"

Determined to avoid any interruption of this highly important occasion, she began to climb the ratlines, on her way to her favorite perch at the mast-head. Each time she moved an arm or a leg in this simple action, however, it struck her with fresh amusement to find them obeying her so readily. Memory told her, of course, that they had always done so before: but before, she had never realized how surprising this was.

Once settled on her perch, she began examining the skin of her hands with the utmost care: for it was *hers*.

She slipped a shoulder out of the top of her frock; and having peeped in to make sure she really was continuous under her clothes, she shrugged it up to touch her cheek. The contact of her face and the warm bare hollow of her shoulder gave her a comfortable thrill, as if it was the caress of some kind friend. But whether the feeling came to her through her cheek or her shoulder, which was the caresser and which the caressed, that no analysis could tell her.

Once fully convinced of this astonishing fact, that she was now Emily Bas-Thornton (why she inserted the "now" she did not know, for she certainly imagined no transmigrational nonsense of having been any one else before), she began seriously to reckon its implications.

First, what agency had so ordered it that out of all the people in the world who she might have been, she was this particular one, this Emily: born in such-and-such a year out of all the years in Time, and encased in this particular rather pleasing little casket of flesh? Had she chosen herself, or had God done it?

At this, another consideration: who was God? She had heard a terrible lot about Him, always: but the question of His identity had been left vague, as much taken for granted as her own. Wasn't she perhaps God, herself? Was it that she was trying to remember? However, the more she tried, the more it eluded her. (How absurd, to disremember such an important point as whether one was God or not!) So she let it slide: perhaps it would come back to her later.

Secondly, why had all this not occurred to her before? She had been alive for over ten years now, and it had never once entered her head. She felt like a man who suddenly remembers at eleven o'clock at night, sitting in his own arm-chair, that he had accepted an invitation to go out to dinner that night. There is no reason for him to remember it now: but there seems equally little why he should not have remembered it in time to keep his engagement. How could he have sat there all the evening without being disturbed by the slightest misgiving? How could Emily have gone on being Emily for ten years without once noticing this apparently obvious fact?

It must not be supposed that she argued it all out in this ordered, but rather long-winded fashion. Each consideration came to her in a momentary flash, quite innocent of words: and in between her mind lazed along, either thinking of nothing or returning to her bees and the fairy queen. If one added up the total of her periods of conscious thought, it would probably reach something between four and five seconds; nearer five, perhaps; but it was spread out over the best part of an hour.

Well then, granted she was Emily, what were the consequences, besides enclosure in that particular little body (which now began on its own account to be aware of a sort of unlocated itch, most probably somewhere on the right thigh), and lodgment behind a particular pair of eyes?

It implied a whole series of circumstances. In the first place, there was her family, a number of brothers and sisters from whom, before, she had never entirely dissociated herself; but now she got such a sudden feeling of being a discrete person that they seemed as separate from her as the ship itself. However, willy-nilly she was almost as tied to them as she was to her body. And then there was this voyage, this ship, this mast round which she had wound her legs. She began to examine it with almost as vivid an illumination as she had studied the skin of her hands. And when she came down from the mast, what would she find at the bottom? There would be Jonsen, and Otto, and the crew: the whole fabric of a daily life which up to now she had accepted as it came, but which now seemed vaguely disquieting. What was going to happen? Were there disasters running about loose, disasters which her rash marriage to the body of Emily Thornton made her vulnerable to?

A sudden terror struck her: did any one know? (Know, I mean, that she was some one in particular, Emily—perhaps even God—not just any little girl.) She could not tell why, but the idea terrified her. It would be bad enough if they should discover she was a particular person—but if they should discover she was God! At all costs she must hide *that* from them.—But suppose they knew already, had simply been hiding it from her (as guardians might from an infant king)? In that case, as in the other, the only thing to do was to continue to behave as if she did not know, and so outwit them.

But if she was God, why not turn all the sailors into white mice, or strike Margaret blind, or cure somebody, or do some other Godlike act of the kind? Why should she hide it? She never really asked herself why: but instinct prompted her strongly of the necessity. Of course, there was the element of doubt (suppose she had made a mistake, and the miracle missed fire): but more largely it was the feeling that she would be able to deal with the situation so much better when she was a little older. Once she had declared herself there would be no turning back; it was much better to keep her godhead up her sleeve for the present.

Grown-ups embark on a life of deception with considerable misgiving, and generally fail. But not so children. A child can hide the most appalling secret without the least effort, and is practically secure against detection. Parents, finding that they see through their child in so many places the child does not know of, seldom realize that, if there is some point the child really gives his mind to hiding, their chances are nil.

So Emily had no misgivings when she determined to preserve her secret, and needed have none.

Down below on the deck the smaller children were repeatedly crowding themselves into a huge coil of rope, feigning sleep and then suddenly leaping out with yelps of panic and dancing round it in consternation and dismay. Emily watched them with that impersonal attention one gives to a kaleidoscope. Presently Harry spied her, and gave a hail.

"Emilee-ee! Come down and play House-on-fire!"

At that, her normal interests momentarily revived. Her stomach as it were leapt within her sympathetically toward the game. But it died in her as suddenly; and not only died, but she did not even feel disposed to waste her noble voice on them. She continued to stare without making any reply whatever.

"Come on!" shouted Edward.

"Come and play!" shouted Laura. "Don't be a pig!"

Then in the ensuing stillness Rachel's voice floated up: "Don't call her, Laura, we don't really want her."

II

But Emily was completely unaffected—only glad that for the present they were all right by themselves. She was already beginning to feel the charge of the party a burden.

It had automatically devolved on her with the defection of Margaret.

It was puzzling, this Margaret business. She could not understand it, and it disturbed her. It dated back really to that night, about a week ago, when she herself had so unaccountably bitten the captain. The memory of her own extraordinary behavior gave her now quite a little shiver of alarm.

Everybody had been very drunk that night, and making a terrible racket—it was impossible to get to sleep. So at last Edward had asked her to tell them a story. But she was not feeling "storyable," so they had asked Margaret; all except Rachel, who had begged Margaret not to, because she wanted to think, she said. But Margaret had been very pleased at being asked, and had begun a very stupid story about a princess who had lots and lots of clothes and was always beating her servant for making mistakes and shutting him up in a dark cupboard. The whole story, really, had been nothing but clothes and beating, and Rachel had *begged* her to stop.

In the middle, a sort of rabble of sailors had come down the ladder, very slowly and with much discussion. They stood at the bottom in a knot, swaying a little and all turned inwards on one of their number. It was so dark one could not see who this was. They were urging him to do something—he hanging back.

"Oh, damn it!" he cried in a thick voice. "Bring me a light, I can't see where dey are!"

It was the voice of the captain—but how altered! There was a sort of suppressed excitement in it. Some one lit a lantern and held it up in the middle. Captain Jonsen stood on his legs half like a big sack of flour, half like a waiting tiger.

"What do you want?" Emily had asked kindly.

But Captain Jonsen stood irresolute, shifting his weight from foot to foot as if he was steering.

"You're drunk, aren't you?" Rachel had piped, loudly and disapprovingly.

But it was Margaret who had behaved most queerly. She had gone yellow as cheese, and her eyes large with terror. She was shivering from head to foot as if she had the fever. It was absurd. Then Emily remembered how stupidly frightened Margaret had been the very first night on the schooner.

At that moment Jonsen had staggered up to Emily, and putting one hand under her chin had begun to stroke her hair with the other. A sort of blind vertigo seized her: she caught his thumb and bit as hard as she could: then, terrified at her own madness, dashed across the hold to where the other children were gathered in a wondering knot.

"What *have* you done!" cried Laura, pushing her away angrily: "Oh you wicked girl, you've hurt him!"

Jonsen was stamping about, swearing and sucking his thumb. Edward had produced a handkerchief, and between them all they had managed to tie it up. He stood staring at the bandaged member for a few moments: shook his head like a wet retriever and retreated on deck, dang-danging under his breath. Margaret had then been so sick they thought she must really have caught fever, and they couldn't get any sense out of her at all.

As Emily, with her new-found consciousness, recapitulated the scene, it was like re-reading a story in a book, so little responsibility did she feel for the merely mechanical creature who had bitten the captain's thumb. Nor was she even very interested: it had been queer, but then there was very little in life which didn't seem queer, now.

As for Jonsen, he and Emily had avoided each other ever since, by mutual consent. She indeed had been in Coventry with everybody for biting him; none of the other children would play with her all the next day, and she recognized that she thoroughly deserved it—it was a *mad* thing to have done. And yet Jonsen, in avoiding her, had himself more the air of being ashamed than angry . . . which was unaccountable.

But what interested her more was the curious way Margaret had gone on, those next few days.

For some time she had behaved very oddly indeed. At first she seemed exaggeratedly frightened of all the men: but then she had suddenly taken to following them about the deck like a dog—not Jonsen, it is true, but Otto especially. Then suddenly she had departed from them altogether and taken up her quarters in the cabin. The curious thing was that now she avoided them all utterly, and spent all her time with the sailors: and the sailors, for their part, seemed to take peculiar pains not only not to let her speak to, but even not to let her be seen by the other children.

Now they hardly saw her at all: and when they did she seemed so different they hardly recognized her: though where the difference lay it would be hard to say.

Emily, from her perch at the mast-head, could just see the girl's head now, through the cabin skylight. Further forward, José had joined the children at their game, and was crawling about on hands and knees with all of them on his back—a fire-engine, of course, such as they had seen in the illustrated magazines from England.

"Emily!" called Harry: "Come and play!"

Down with a rush fell the curtain on all Emily's cogitations. In a second she was once more a happy little animal—*any* happy little animal. She slid down the shrouds like a real sailor, and in no time was directing the fire-fighting operations as imperiously as any other of this brigade of superintendents.

III

That night in the Parliament of Beds there was raised at last a question which you may well be surprised had not been raised before. Emily had just reduced her family to silence by sheer ferocity, when Harry's rapid, nervous, lisping voice piped up:

"Emily Emily may I ask you a question, please?"

"Go to sleep!"

There was a moment's whispered confabulation.

"But it's very important, please, and we all want to know."

"What?"

"Are these people pirates?"

Emily sat bolt upright with astonishment.

"Of course not!"

Harry sounded rather crestfallen.

"I don't know . . . I just thought they might . . ."

"But they *are*!" declared Rachel firmly. "Margaret told me!"

"Nonsense!" said Emily. "There aren't any pirates nowadays."

"Margaret said," went on Rachel, "that time we were shut up on the other ship she heard one of the sailors calling out pirates had come on board."

Emily had an inspiration.

"No, you silly, he must have said *pilots*."

"What are pilots?" asked Laura.

"They Come On Board," explained Emily, lamely. "Don't you remember that picture in the dining-room at home, called The Pilot Comes On Board?"

Laura listened with rapt attention. The explanation of what pilots were was not very illuminating; but then she did not know what pirates were either. So you might think the whole discussion meant very little to her, but there you would be wrong: the question was evidently important to the older ones, therefore she gave her whole mind to listening.

The pirate heresy was considerably shaken. How could they say for certain which word Margaret had really heard? Rachel changed sides.

"They can't be pirates," she said. "Pirates are wicked."

"Couldn't we ask them?" Edward persisted.

Emily considered.

"I don't think it would be very polite."

"I'm sure they wouldn't mind," said Edward. "They're awfully decent."

"I think they mightn't like it," said Emily. In her heart she was afraid of the answer; and if they were pirates, it would here again be better to pretend not to know.

"I know!" she said. "Shall I ask the Mouse with the Elastic Tail?"

"Yes, do!" cried Laura. It was months since the oracle

had been consulted; but her faith was still perfect.

Emily communed with herself in a series of short squeaks.

"He says they are *Pilots*," she announced.

"Oh," said Edward deeply: and they all went to sleep.

7

EDWARD OFTEN THOUGHT, as he strode scowling up and down the deck by himself, that this was exactly the life for him. What a lucky boy he was, to have tumbled into it by good fortune, instead of having to run away to sea as most other people did! In spite of the White Mouse's pronouncement (whom secretly he had long ceased to believe in), he had no doubt that this was a pirate vessel: and no doubt either that when presently Jonsen was killed in some furious battle the sailors would unanimously elect him their captain.

The girls were a great nuisance. A ship was no place for them. When he was captain he would have them marooned.

Yet there had been a time when he had wished he was

a girl himself. "When I was young," he once confided to the admiring Harry, "I used to think girls were bigger and stronger than boys. Weren't I silly?"

"Yes," said Harry.

Harry did not confide it to Edward, but he also, *now*, wished he was a girl. It was not for the same reason: younger than Edward, he was still at the amorous age; and because he found the company of girls almost magically pleasing, fondly imagined it would be even more so if he were one himself. He was always finding himself, for being a boy, shut out from their most secret councils. Emily of course was too old to count as female in his eyes: but to Rachel and Laura he was indiscriminately devoted. When Edward was captain, he would be mate: and when he imagined this future, it consisted for the most part in rescuing Rachel—or Laura, *n'importe*—from new and complicated dangers.

They were all by now just as much at home on the schooner as they had been in Jamaica. Indeed, nothing very continuous was left of Ferndale for the youngest ones: only a number of luminous pictures of quite unimportant incidents. Emily of course remembered most things, and could put them together. The death of Tabby, for instance: she would never forget that as long as she lived. She could recollect, too, that Ferndale had tumbled down flat. And her Earthquake: she had been in an earthquake, and could remember every detail of *that*. Had it been as a result of the earthquake that Ferndale had tumbled down? That sounded likely. There had been quite a high wind at that time, too. . . . She could remember that they had all been bathing when the earthquake had come, and then had ridden somewhere on ponies. But they had been *in* the house when it fell down: she was pretty sure of that. It was all a little difficult to join up.—Then, when was it she had found that negro village? She could remember with a startling clearness bending down and feeling among the bamboo roots for the bubbling spring, then looking round and seeing the black children scampering away up the clearing. That must have been years and years ago. But clearer than everything was that awful night when Tabby had stalked up and down the room, his eyes blazing and his fur twitching, his voice melodious with tragedy, until those horrible black shapes had flown in through the fanlight and savaged him out into the bush. The horror of the scene was even increased because it had once or twice come back to her in dreams, and because when she dreamt it (though it seemed the same) there was always some frightful difference. One night (and that was the worst of all) she had rushed out to rescue him, when her darling faithful Tabby had come up to her with the same horrible look on his face the captain had worn that time she bit his thumb, and had chased her down avenues and avenues and avenues and avenues of cabbage-palms, with Exeter House at the end of them never getting any nearer however much she ran. She knew, of course, it was not the real Tabby, but a sort of diabolic double: and Margaret had sat up an orange tree jeering at her, gone as black as a negro.

One of the drawbacks of life at sea was the cockroaches. They were winged. They infested the fore-hold, and the smell they made was horrible. One had to put up with them. But one didn't do much washing at sea: and it was a common thing to wake up in the morning and find the brutes had gnawed the quick from under one's nails, or gnawed all the hard skin off the soles of one's feet, so that one could hardly walk. Anything in the least greasy or dirty they set on at once. Button-holes were their especial delight. One did little washing: fresh water was too valuable, and salt water had practically no effect. From handling tarry ropes and greasy ironwork their hands would have disgraced a slum-child. There is a sailor saying which includes a peck of dirt in the mariner's monthly rations: but the children on the schooner must have often consumed far more.

Not that it was a dirty ship—the fo'c'sle probably was, but the Nordicism of captain and mate kept the rest looking clean enough. But even the cleanest-looking ship is seldom clean to the touch. Their clothes José washed occasionally with his own shirt: and in that climate they were dry again by the morning.

Jamaica had faded into the past: England, to which they had supposed they were going, and of which a very curious picture had formerly been built up in their minds by their parents' constant references to it, receded again into the mists of myth. They lived in the present, adapted themselves to it, and might have been born in a hammock and christened at a binnacle before they had been there many weeks. They seemed to have no natural fear of heights, and the farther they were above the deck, the happier. On a calm day Edward used to hang by his knees from the cross-trees in order to feel the blood run into his head. The flying-jib, too, which was usually down, made an admirable cocoon for hide-and-seek: one took a firm grip of the hanks and robands, and swathed oneself in the canvas. Once, suspecting Edward was hidden there, instead of going out on the jib-boom to look, the other children cast off the down-haul and then all together gave a great tug at the halyard which nearly pitched him into the sea. The shark myth is greatly exaggerated: it is untrue, for instance, that they can take a leg clean off at the hip—their bite is a tearing one, not a clean cut: and a practiced bather can keep them off easily with a welt on the nose each time they turn over to strike[1]: but all the same, once overboard there would have been little hope for a small boy

---

1. The tiger-shark of the South Seas is of course a very different cattle.

like Edward: and a severe wigging they all got for their prank.

Often several of those thick, rubber-like protuberances would follow the vessel for hours—perhaps in the hope of just some such antic.

Sharks were not without their uses, however: it is well known that Catch a Shark Catch a Breeze, so when a breeze was needed the sailors baited a big hook and presently hauled one on board with the winch. The bigger he was, the better breeze was hoped for: and his tail was nailed to the jib-boom. One day they got a great whacking fellow on board, and having cut off his jaw some one heaved it into the ship's latrine (which no one was so lubberly as to use for its proper purpose) and thought no more about it. One wildish night, however, old José did go there, and sat full on that wicked *cheval de frise*. He yelled like a madman: and the crew were better pleased than they had been with any joke that year, and even Emily thought if only it had been less improper how funny it would have been. It would certainly have puzzled an archaeologist, faced with José's mummy, to guess how he came by those curious scars.

The ship's monkey also added a lot to the ship's merriment. One day some sucker-fish had fixed themselves firmly to the deck, and he undertook to dislodge them. After a few preliminary tugs, he braced three legs and his tail against the deck and lunged like a madman. But they would not budge. The crew were standing round in a ring, and he felt his honor was at stake: somehow, they *must* be removed. So, disgusting though they must have tasted to a vegetarian, he set to and ate them, right down to the sucker, and was loudly applauded.

Edward and Harry often talked over how they would distinguish themselves in the next engagement. Sometimes they would rehearse it: storm the galley with uncouth shouts, or spring into the main rigging and order every one to be thrown into the sea. Once, as they went into battle,

"I am armed with a sword and a pistol!" chanted Edward:

"And I am armed with a key and half a whist-le!" chanted the more literal Harry.

They took care to hold those rehearsals when the real pirates were out of the way: it was not so much that they feared the criticism of the professional eye as that it was not yet openly recognized what they were; and all the children shared Emily's instinct that it was better to pretend not to know—a sort of magical belief, at bottom.

Although Laura and Rachel were thrown together a great deal, and were all one goddess to Harry, their inner lives differed in almost every respect. It was a matter of principle, as will have been noticed, for them to disagree on every point: but it was a matter of nature too. Rachel had only two activities. One was domestic. She was never happy unless surrounded by the full paraphernalia of a household: she left houses and families wherever she went. She collected bits of oakum and the moltings of a worn-out mop, wrapped them in rags and put them to sleep in every nook and cranny. *Guai*, who woke one of her twenty or thirty babies—worse still, should he clear it away! She could even summon up maternal feelings for a marline-spike, and would sit up aloft rocking it in her arms and crooning. The sailors avoided walking underneath: for such an infant, if dropped from a height, will find its way through the thickest skull (an accident which sometimes befalls unpopular captains).

Further, there was hardly an article of ship's use, from the windlass to the bosun's chair, but she had metamorphosed it into some sort of furniture: a table or a bed or a lamp or a tea-set: and marked it as her property: and what she had marked as her property no one might touch—if she could prevent it. To parody Hobbes, she claimed as her own whatever she had mixed her imagination with; and the greater part of her time was spent in angry or tearful assertions of her property-rights.

Her other interest was moral. She had an extraordinary vivid, *simple* sense, that child, of Right and Wrong—it almost amounted to a precocious ethical genius. Every action, her own or any one else's, was immediately judged good or bad, and uncompromisingly praised or blamed. She was never in doubt.

To Emily, Conscience meant something very different. She was still only half aware of that secret criterion within her: but was terrified of it. She had not Rachel's clear divination: she never knew when she might offend this inner harpy, Conscience, unwittingly: and lived in terror of those brazen claws, should she ever let it be hatched from the egg. When she felt its latent strength stir in its pre-natal sleep, she forced her mind to other things, and would not even let herself recognize her fear of it. But she knew, at the bottom of her heart she *knew*, that one day some action of hers would rouse it, something awful done quite unwittingly would send it raging round her soul like a whirlwind. She might go weeks together in a happy unconsciousness, she might have flashes of vision when she knew she was God Himself: but at the same time she knew, beyond all doubt, in her innermost being, that she was damned, that there never had been any one as wicked as her since the world began.

Not so Rachel: to her, Conscience was by no means so depressing an affair. It was simply a comfortable mainspring of her life, smooth-working, as pleasant as a healthy appetite. For instance, it was now tacitly admitted that all these men were pirates. That is, they were wicked. It therefore devolved on her to convert them: and she entered on her plans for this without a shadow either of misgiving or reluctance. Her conscience gave her no pain because it never occurred to her as conceivable that she should do anything but follow its dictates, or fail to see them clearly. She would try and convert these people first: probably they would reform, but if they did not—well, she would send for the police. Since either result was right, it mattered not at all which Circumstance should call for.

So much for Rachel. The inside of Laura was different indeed: something vast, complicated, and nebulous that can hardly be put into language. To take a metaphor from tadpoles, though legs were growing her gills had not yet dropped off. Being nearly four years old, she was certainly a child: and children are human (if one allows the term "human" a wide sense): but she had not altogether ceased to be a baby: and babies of course are not human—they are animals, and have a very ancient and ramified culture, as cats have, and fishes, and even snakes: the same in kind as these, but much more complicated and vivid, since babies are, after all, one of the most developed species of the lower vertebrates.

In short, babies have minds which work in terms and categories of their own which cannot be translated into the terms and categories of the human mind.

It is true they look human—but not so human, to be quite fair, as many monkeys.

Subconsciously, too, every one recognizes they are animals—why else do people always laugh when a baby does some action resembling the human, as they would at a praying mantis? If the baby was only a less-developed man, there would be nothing funny in it, surely.

Possibly a case might be made out that children are not human either: but I should not accept it. Agreed that their minds are not just more ignorant and stupider than ours, but differ in kind of thinking (are *mad*, in fact): but one can, by an effort of will and imagination, think like a child, at least in a partial degree—and even if one's success is infinitesimal it invalidates the case: while one can no more think like a baby, in the smallest respect, than one can think like a bee.

How then can one begin to describe the inside of Laura, where the child-mind lived in the midst of the familiar relics of the baby-mind, like a Fascist in Rome?

When swimming under water, it is a very sobering thing suddenly to look a large octopus in the face. One never forgets it: one's respect, yet one's feeling of the hopelessness of any real intellectual sympathy. One is soon reduced to mere physical admiration, like any silly painter, of the cow-like tenderness of the eye, of the beautiful and infinitesimal mobility of that large and toothless mouth, which accepts as a matter of course that very water against which you, for your life's sake, must be holding your breath. There he reposes in a fold of rock, apparently weightless in the clear green medium but very large, his long arms, suppler than silk, coiled in repose, or stirring in recognition of your presence. Far above, everything is bounded by the surface of the air, like a bright window of glass. Contact with a small baby can conjure at least an echo of that feeling in those who are not obscured by an uprush of maternity to the brain.

Of course it is not really so cut-and-dried as all this; but often the only way of attempting to express the truth is to build it up, like a card-house, of a pack of lies.

It was only in Laura's inner mind, however, that these elaborate vestiges of babyhood remained: outwardly she appeared fully a child—a rather reserved, odd, and indeed rather captivating one. Her face was not pretty, with its heavy eyebrows and reduced chin: but she had a power of apt movement, the appropriate attitude for every occasion, that was most striking. A child who can show her affection for you, for instance, in the very way she plants her feet on the ground, has a liberal gift of that bodily genius called charm. Actually, this particular one was a rare gesture with her: nine-tenths of her life being spent in her own head, she seldom had time to feel at all strongly either for or against people. The feelings she thus expressed were generally of a more impersonal kind, and would have fascinated an admirer of the ballet: and it was all the more remarkable that she *had* developed a dog-like devotion to the reserved and coarse-looking captain of the pirates.

No one really contends that children have any insight into character: their likings are mostly imaginative, not intuitive. "What do you think I am?" the exasperated ruffian had asked on a famous occasion. One might well ask what Laura thought he was: and there is no means of knowing.

II

Pigs grow quickly, quicker even than children: and much though the latter altered in the first month on board, the little black porker (whose name by the by was Thunder) altered even more. He soon grew to such a size one could not possibly allow him to lie on one's stomach any more: so, as his friendliness did not diminish, the functions were reversed, and it became a common thing to find one child, or a whole bench of them, sitting on his scaly side. They grew very fond of him indeed (especially Emily), and called him their Dear Love, their Only Dear, their Own True Heart, and other names. But he had only two things he ever said. When his back was being scratched he enunciated an occasional soft and happy grunt; and that same phrase (only in a different tone) had to serve for every other occasion and emotion—except one. When a particularly heavy lot of children sat down on him at once, he uttered the faintest ghost of a little moan, as affecting as the wind in a very distant chimney, as if the air in him was being squeezed out through a pin-hole.

One cannot wish for a more comfortable seat than an acquiescent pig.

"If I was the Queen," said Emily, "I should most certainly have a pig for a throne."

"Perhaps she has," suggested Harry.

"He *does* like being scratched," she added presently in a very sentimental tone, as she rubbed his scurfy back.

The mate was watching:

"I should think *you*'d like being scratched, if your skin was in that condition!"

"Oh how disGUSTing you are!" cried Emily, delighted.

But the idea took root.

"I don't think I should kiss him quite so much if I was you," Emily presently advised Laura, who was lying with her arms tight round his neck and covering his briny snout with kisses from ring to ears.

"My pet! My love!" murmured Laura, by way of indirect protest.

The wily mate had foreseen that some estrangement

would be necessary if they were ever to have fresh pork served without salt tears. He intended this to be the thin end of the wedge. But alas! Laura's mind was as humorsome an instrument to play as the Twenty-three-stringed Lute.

When dinner-time came, the children mustered for their soup and biscuit.

They were not overfed on the schooner: they were given little that is generally considered wholesome, or to contain vitamines (unless these lurked in the aforesaid peck of dirt): but they seemed none the worse. First the cook boiled the various non-perishable vegetables they carried in a big pot together for a couple of hours. Then a lump of salt beef from the cask forward, having been rinsed in a little fresh water, was added, and allowed to simmer with the rest till it was just cooked. Then it was withdrawn, and the captain and mate ate their soup first and their meat afterwards, out of plates, like gentlemen. After that, if it was a week-day, the meat was put to cool on the cabin shelf, ready to warm up in to-morrow's soup, and the crew and children ate the liquor with biscuit: but if it was Sunday, the captain took the lump of meat and with a benevolent air cut it up in small pieces, as if indeed for a nursery, and mixed it up with the vegetables in the huge wooden bowl out of which crew and children all dipped. It was a very patriarchal way of feeding.

Even at dinner Margaret did not join the others, but ate in the cabin; though there were only two plates on the whole ship. Probably she used the mate's when he had finished.

Laura and Rachel fought that day to tears over a particularly succulent piece of yam. Emily let them. To make those two agree was a task she was wise not to undertake. Besides, she was very busy over her own dinner. Edward managed to silence them, however, by declaring in a most terrible voice: "Shut up or I'll SABER you!"

Emily's estrangement from the captain had reached by now a rather uncomfortable stage. When these things are fresh and new the two parties avoid meeting, and all is well: but after some days they are apt to forget, find themselves on the point of chatting, and then suddenly remember that they are not on speaking terms and have to retire in confusion. Nothing can be more uncomfortable for a child. The difficulty of effecting a reconciliation in this case was that both parties felt wholly in the wrong. Each repented the impulse of a momentary insanity, and neither had an inkling the other felt the same: thus each waited for the other to show signs of forgiveness. Moreover, while the captain had far the more serious reason for being ashamed of himself, Emily was naturally far the more sensitive and concerned of the two: so it about balanced. Thus, if Emily rushed blithely up to the captain embracing a flying-fish, caught his eye and slunk round the other side of the galley, he put it down to a permanent feeling of condemnation and re-pulsion: blushed a deep purple and stared stonily at his wrinkling mainsail—and Emily wondered if he was *never* going to forget that bitten thumb.

But this afternoon things came to a head. Laura was trotting about behind him, striking her attitudes. Edward had at last discovered which was windward and which was leeward, and had come hot-foot to learn the first of the Sovereign Rules of Life: and Emily, with one of her wretched lapses of memory, was all agog at his elbow.

Edward was duly catechized and passed.

"Dis is the first rule," said the captain: "*Never throw anything to windward except hot water or ashes.*"

Edward's face developed exactly the look of bewilder-ment that was intended.

"But *windward* is . . ." he began: "I mean, wouldn't they blow . . ." then he stopped, wondering if he had got the terms the right way round after all. Jonsen was delighted at the success of this ancient joke. Emily, trying to stand on one leg, bewildered also, lost her balance and clutched at Jonsen's arm. He looked at her—they all looked at her.

Much the best way of escaping from an embarrassing rencontre, when to walk away would be an impossible strain on the nerves, is to retire in a series of somersaults.

Emily immediately started turning head over heels up the deck.

It was very difficult to keep direction, and the giddiness was appalling; but she *must* keep it up till she was out of sight, or die.

Just then, Rachel, who was up the mainmast, dropped, for the first time, her marline-spike. She uttered a terrible shriek—for what *she* saw was a baby falling to dash its brains out on the deck.

Jonsen gave an ineffectual little grunt of alarm—men can never learn to give a full-bodied scream like a woman.

But Emily gave the most desperate yell of all, though several seconds after the other two: for the wicked steel stood quivering in the deck, having gouged a track through her calf on the way. Her wrought-up nerves and sickening giddiness joined with the shock and pain to give a heart-rending poignancy to her crying. Jonsen was by her in a second, caught her up, and carried her, sobbing miserably, down into the cabin. There sat Margaret, bending over some mending, her slim shoulders hunched up, humming softly and feeling deadly ill.

"Get out!" said Jonsen, in a low, brutal voice. Without a word or sign Margaret gathered up her sewing and climbed on deck.

Jonsen smeared some Stockholm tar on a rag, and bound up Emily's leg with more than a little skill, though

the tar of course was agonizing to her. She had cried herself right out by the time he laid her in his bunk. When
she opened her streaming eyes and saw him bending over
her, nothing in his clumsy face but concern and an almost overpowering pity, she was so full of joy at being at
last forgiven that she reached up her arms and kissed
him. He sat down on the locker, rocking himself backwards and forwards gently. Emily dozed for a few minutes: when she woke up he was still there.

"Tell me about when you were little," she said.

Jonsen sat on, silent, trying to project his unwieldy
mind back into the past.

"When I was a boy," he said at last, "it wasn't thought
lucky to grease your own sea-boots. My Auntie used to
grease mine before we went out with the lugger."

He paused for some time.

"We divided the fish up into six shares—one for the
boat, and one for each of us."

That was all. But it was of the greatest interest to
Emily, and she shortly fell asleep again, supremely happy.

So for several days the captain and mate had to share
the latter's bunk, Box-and-Cox; Heaven knows what hole
Margaret was banished to. The gash in Emily's leg was
one which would take some time to heal. To make things
worse, the weather became very unsteady: when she was
awake she was all right, but if she fell asleep she began to

roll about the bunk, and then, of course, the pain waked her again; which soon reduced her to a feverish and nervous condition, although the leg itself was going on as well as could be expected. The other children, of course, used to come and see her: but they did not enjoy it much, as there was nothing to do down in the cabin, once the novelty of admittance to the Holy Place had worn off. So their visits were perfunctory and short. They must have had a high old time at night, however, by themselves in the fore-hold, now that the cat was away. They looked like it, too, in the mornings.

Otto used sometimes to come and teach her to make fancy knots, and at the same time pour out his grievances against the captain: though these latter were always received with an uncomfortable silence. Otto was a Viennese by birth, but had stowed away in a Danube barge when he was ten years old, had taken to the sea, and thereafter generally served in English ships. The only place since his childhood where he had ever spent any considerable time on shore was Wales. For some years he had sailed coastwise from the once-promising harbor of Portdinlleyn, which is now practically dead: and so, as well as German, Spanish, and English, he could talk Welsh fluently. It was not a long residence, but at an impressionable age; and when he talked to Emily of his past it was mostly of his life as a "boy" on the slate-boats. Captain

Jonsen came of a Danish family settled on the Baltic coast, at Lübeck. He too had spent most of his time on English ships. How or when he and Otto had first met, or how they had drifted into the Cuban piracy business, Emily never discovered. They had plainly been inseparable for many years. She preferred letting them ramble on, to asking questions or trying to fit things together: she had that sort of mind.

When the knots palled, José sent her a beautiful crochet-hook he had carved out of a beef bone: and by pulling threads out of a piece of sail-cloth she was able to set to work to crochet doilies for the cabin table. But I am afraid that she also drew a lot, till the whole of the inside of the bunk was soon as thoroughly scribbled over as a paleolithic cave. What the captain would say when he found out was a consideration best postponed. The fun was to find knots, and unevennesses in the paint, that looked like something; and then with a pencil to make them look more like it—putting an eye in the walrus, or supplying the rabbit with his missing ear. That is what artists call having a proper feeling for one's material.

Instead of getting better the weather got worse: and the universe soon became a very unstable place indeed: it became almost impossible to crochet. She had to cling on to the side of the bunk all the time, to prevent her leg getting banged.

It was in this inconvenient weather, however, that the pirates chose at last to make another capture. It turned out not a rich one: a small Dutch steamer, taking a consignment of performing animals to one of Mr. Barnum's predecessors. The captain of the steamer, who was conceited in a way that only certain Dutchmen *can* be conceited, gave them a lot of trouble, in spite of the fact that he had practically nothing worth taking. He was a first-class sailor: but he was very fair, and had no neck. In the end they had to tie him up, bring him on board the schooner, and lay him on the cabin floor where Emily could keep an eye on him. He reeked of some particularly nauseous brand of cigars that made her head swim.

The other children had played quite an important part in the capture. They did far better as a badge of innocuousness than even the "ladies." The steamer (little more than dressed-up sailing-vessels they were then), thoroughly disgruntled at the weather, was wallowing about like a porpoise, her decks awash and her funnel over one ear, so to speak: so when a boat put out from the schooner, its departure cheered lustily by Edward, Harry, Rachel, and Laura, though his pride might resent it, the Dutchman never thought of suspecting this presumable offer of assistance, and let them come on board.

It was then he began to give trouble, and they had to

remove him onto the schooner. Their tempers were none too good on finding their booty was a lion, a tiger, two bears, and a lot of monkeys: so it is quite likely they were none too gentle with him in transit.

The next thing was to discover whether the *Thelma*, like the *Clorinda*, carried another, a secret cargo of greater value. They had imprisoned all the crew, now, aft: so one by one they were brought up on deck and questioned. But either there was no money on board, or the crew did not know of it, or would not tell. Most of them, indeed, appeared frightened enough to have sold their grandmothers: but some of them simply laughed at the pirates' bogey-bogey business, guessing they drew the line at murder in cold blood, sober.

What was done in each case was the same. When each man was finished with he was sent forward and shut in the fo'c'sle: and before bringing another up from aft one of the pirates would unmercifully belabor a roll of sail-cloth with a cat-o'-nine-tails while another yelled like the damned. Then a shot was fired in the air, and something thrown overboard to make a splash. All this, of course, was to impress those still down in the cabin awaiting their turns: and the pretense was quite as effective as the reality could have been. But it did no good, since probably there was no treasure to disclose.

There was, however, a plentiful supply of Dutch

spirits and liqueurs on board: and these the pirates found a welcome change after so much West Indian rum.

After they had been drinking them for an hour or two Otto had a brilliant idea. Why not give the children a circus? They had begged and begged to be taken onto the steamer to see the animals. Well, why not stage something really magnificent for them—a fight between the lion and the tiger, for instance?

No sooner said than done. The children, and every man who could be spared, came onto the steamer, and took up positions at safe heights in the rigging. The cargo-gaff was rigged, the hatch opened, and the two iron cages, with their stale cat-like reek, were hauled up on deck. Then the little Malay keepers, who kept twittering to each other in their windy tones, were made to open them, that the two monarchs of the jungle might come out and do battle.

How they were to be got in again was a question that never occurred to any one's consideration. Yet it is generally supposed to be easier to let tigers out of cages than to put them back.

In this case, however, even when the cages were open, neither of the beasts seemed very anxious to get out. They lay on the floor growling (or groaning) slightly, but making no move except to roll their eyes.

It was very unfortunate for poor Emily that she was

missing all this, laid by the leg in Jonsen's stuffy cabin with the Dutch captain to guard.

When at first they had been left alone together he had tried to speak to her: but unlike so many Dutchmen he did not know a word of English. He could just move his head, and he kept turning his eyes first on a very sharp knife which some idiot had dropped in a corner of the cabin floor, then on Emily. He was asking her to get it for him, of course.

But Emily was terrified of him. There is something much more frightening about a man who is tied up than a man who is not tied up—I suppose it is the fear he may get loose.

The feeling of not being able to get out of the bunk and escape added the true nightmare panic.

Remember that he had no neck, and the cigar-reek.

At last he must have caught the look of fear and disgust in her face, where he had expected compassion. He began to act for himself. First gently rocking his bound body from side to side, he set himself to roll.

Emily screamed for help, beating with her fist on the bunk: but none came. Even the sailors who were left on board were out of ear-shot: they were straining all their attention to see what was happening on the steamer that wallowed and heaved seventy yards away. There, one of the pirates, greatly daring, had descended to the rail and begun throwing belaying-pins at the cages, to rouse their occupants. If the beasts so much as lashed their tails in response, however, he would scuttle up any rope like a frightened mouse. Only the Malay keepers remained permanently on deck, taking no notice: sitting on their heels in a ring and crooning discordantly through their noses. Probably they felt inside much as the lion and tiger did.

After some minutes, however, the pirates grew bolder. Otto came right up to one cage, and started poking the tiger's ribs with a hand-spike. But the poor beast was far too sea-sick to be roused even by that. Gradually the whole crowd of the spectators descended onto the deck and stood round, still not unprepared to bolt, while the drunk mate, and even Captain Jonsen (who was perfectly sober), goaded and jeered.

It was not surprising no one heard poor Emily, left alone in the cabin with the terrible Dutchman.

She screamed and screamed: but there was no awakening from *this* nightmare.

By now he had managed to roll himself, in spite of the motion of the vessel, almost within reach of the coveted knife. The veins on his forehead stood out with his exertion and the stricture of his bonds. His fingers were groping, behind his back, for the edge.

Emily, beside herself with terror, suddenly became possessed by the strength of despair. In spite of the agony it caused her leg she flung herself out of the bunk, and just managed to seize the knife before he could maneuver his bound hands within reach of it.

In the course of the next five seconds she had slashed and jabbed at him in a dozen places: then, flinging the knife towards the door, somehow managed to struggle back into the bunk.

The Dutchman, bleeding rapidly, blinded with his own blood, lay still and groaned. Emily, her own wound re-opened, and overcome with pain and terror, fainted. The knife, flung wildly, missed its aim and clattered down the steps again onto the cabin floor: and the first witness of the scene was Margaret, who presently peered down from the deck above, her dulled eyes standing out from her small, skull-like face.

AS FOR JONSEN and Otto, unable by other means to rouse the dormant animals, they collected their men and with big levers managed to tilt the cages, spilling the beasts out onto the deck.

But not even so would they fight—or even show signs of resentment. As they had lain and groaned in their cages, so they now lay and groaned on the deck.

They were small specimens of their kind, and emaci-ated by travel. Otto with a sudden oath seized the tiger round its middle and hauled it upright on its hind legs: Jonsen did the same by the more top-heavy lion: and so the two principals to the duel faced each other, their heads lolling over the arms of their seconds.

But in the eyes of the tiger a slight ember of conscious-ness seemed to smolder. Suddenly it tautened its mus-cles: a slight effort, yet it burst from the merely human grip of Otto like Samson from the new ropes—nearly dis-located his arms before he had time to let go. Quicker than eye could see, it had cuffed him, rending half his face. Tigers are no plaything. Jonsen dropped the huge bulk of the lion on top of it, and escaped with Otto through an open door: while the pirates, tumbling over each other like peo-ple in a burning theater, struggled to get back in the rigging.

The lion rolled clear. The tiger, lurching unsteadily, crept back into its cage. The keening Malays took no notice of the whole scene.

And yet, what a scene it had been!

But now the heroic circus was over. Chastened, bruised by each other in their panic, the drunken pirates helped the mate into the first of the two boats, and pulling hel-ter-skelter in the choppy sea, returned to the schooner. One by one they climbed the rail and vaulted on deck.

Sailors have keen noses. They smelt blood at once, and crowded round the companion-way: where Margaret still sat, as if numb, on the top step.

Emily lay in the bunk below, her eyes shut—conscious again, but her eyes shut.

The Dutch captain they could see on the floor, stretched in a pool of blood. *"But, Gentlemen, I have a wife and children!"* he suddenly said in Dutch, in a surprised and gentle tone: then died, not so much of any mortal wound as of the number of superficial gashes he had received.

IT WAS PLAINLY Margaret who had done it—killed a bound, defenseless man, for no reason at all; and now sat watching him die, with her dull, meaningless stare.

8

THE CONTEMPT THEY already felt for Margaret, their complete lack of pity in her obvious illness and misery, had been in direct proportion to the childhood she had belied.

This crime would have seemed to them grave on the part of a grown man, in its unrelieved wantonness: but done by one of her years, and nurture, it was unspeakable. She was lifted by the arms from the stair where she still sat, and without a moment's hesitation (other than that resulting from too many helping hands) was dropped into the sea.

But yet the expression of her face, as—like the big white pig in the squall—she vanished to windward, left a picture in Otto's mind he never forgot. She was, after all, his affair.

The Dutchman's body was fetched up on deck. Captain Jonsen went below: and once bent over poor little Emily. She only screwed up her eyes tighter, when she felt his hot breath on her face. She did not open them till everybody had quite gone—and shut them again when presently José came to swab the cabin floor.

THE SECOND BOAT, bringing back the rest of the crew and the four children, almost ran into Margaret before they saw her. She was swimming desperately, but in complete silence: her hair now plastered across her eyes and mouth, now floating out on the water as her head went under. They lifted her into the boat and set her in the stern-sheets with the other children. So it was they found themselves together again.

In her sopping condition, the others naturally gave her elbow-room: but still, she was among them. They sat and stared at her, their eyes very wide and serious, but without speaking. Margaret, her teeth chattering with exhaustion, tried ineffectually to wring out the hem of her frock. She did not speak either: but nevertheless it was not long before both she and the other children felt a sort of thaw setting in between them.

As to the oarsmen, they never troubled their heads as to how she came in the water. They supposed she had accidentally slipped over the side: but were not particularly interested, especially as they had their work cut out maneuvering round to the schooner's lee and clambering on board. There was a tremendous pow-wow going on aft, so that no one noticed them arrive.

Once on board, Margaret went straight forward as of old, climbed down the ladder into the forehold and undressed, the other children watching her every movement with an unfeigned interest. Then she rolled herself in a blanket, and lay down.

They none of them noticed quite how it happened: but in less than half an hour they were all five absorbed in a game of Consequences. Presently one of the crew came, peered down the hatch and then shouted "Yes!" to the rest, and then went away again. But they neither saw nor heard him.

From now on, however, the atmosphere of the schooner suffered a change. A murder is inclined to have this effect on a small community. As a matter of fact, the Dutch captain's was the first blood to be shed on board, in the course of business at any rate (I will not answer for private quarrels). The way it had been shed left the pirates profoundly shocked, their eyes opened to a depravity of human nature they had not dreamt of: but also it gave them an uncomfortable feeling round the neck. So long as there was only the circus-prank to avenge, no American man-of-war was likely to be dispatched in their pursuit: high Naval Authorities shrink naturally from any contact with the ridiculous: but suppose the steamer put into port, and announced the forcible abduction of her captain? Or worse, suppose her mate, with an accursed spyglass, had seen that captain's bloody body take its last dive? Pursuit would be only too likely.

The plea "It was none of us men did this wicked deed, but one of our young female prisoners," was hardly one which could be submitted to a jury.

Captain Jonsen had discovered from the steamer's log where he was: so he put the schooner about, and set a course for his refuge at Santa Lucia. It was unlikely, he thought, now, that any British man-of-war would still be cruising about the scene of the *Clorinda* episode—they had too much to do: and he had reasons (fairly expensive ones) for not anticipating any molestation from the Spanish authorities. He did not like going home with an empty ship, of course: but that appeared inevitable.

The outward sign of this change in the atmosphere of the schooner was a spontaneous increase in the strictness of discipline. Not a drop of rum was drunk. Watch was kept with the regularity of a line-of-battle ship. The schooner became tidier, more seamanlike in every way.

Thunder was slain and eaten the next day, without any regard for the feelings of his lovers: indeed, all tenderness towards the children vanished. Even José ceased playing with them. They were treated with a detached severity not wholly divorced from fear—as if these unfortunate men at last realized what diabolic yeast had been introduced into their lump.

So sensible were the children themselves of the change that they even forgot to mourn for Thunder—excepting Laura, whose face burned an angry red for half a day.

But the ship's monkey, on the other hand, with no pig now to tease, nearly died of ennui.

II

The reopening of the wound in her leg made it several days more before Emily was fit to be moved from the cabin. During this time she was much alone. Jonsen and Otto seldom came below, and when they did were too preoccupied to heed her blandishing. She sang, and conversed to herself, almost incessantly; only interrupting herself to beseech these two, with a superfluity of endearments, to pick up her crochet-hook, to look at the animal she had built out of her blanket, to tell her a story, to tell her what naughty things they did when they were little—how unlike Emily it was, all this gross bidding for attention ! But as a rule they went away again, or went to sleep, without taking the least notice of her.

As well, she told herself, *to* herself, endless stories: as many as there are in *The Arabian Nights*, and quite as involved. But the strings of words she used to utter aloud had nothing to do with this: I mean, that when she made a sort of narrative noise (which was often), she did it for the noise's sake: the silent, private formation of sentences and scenes, in one's head, is far preferable for real story-telling. If you had been watching her then, unseen, you could only have told she was doing it by the dramatic expressions of her face, and her restless flexing and tossing—and if she had had the slightest inkling you were there, the audible rigmarole would have started again. (No one who has private thoughts going on loudly in his own head is quite sure of their not being overheard unless he is providing something else to occupy foreign ears.)

When she sang, however, it was always wordless: an endless succession of notes, like a bird's, fixed to the first vocable handy, and practically without tune. Not being musical, there was never any reason for her to stop: so one song would often go on for half an hour.

Although José had scrubbed the cabin floor as well as he could, a large stain still remained.

At times she let her mind wander about, quite peacefully, in her memories of Jamaica: a period which now seemed to her very remote, a golden age. How young she must have been! When her imagination grew tired, too, she could recall the Anansi stories Old Sam had told her: and they often proved the point of departure for new ones of her own.

Also she could remember the creepy things he had told her about duppies. *How* they used to tease the negroes about the supposed duppy at the bathing-hole, the duppy of the drowned man! It gave one an enormous sense of power, that—not to believe in duppies.

But she found herself taking much less pleasure in duppies now than she used.

She even once caught herself wondering what the Dutchman's duppy would look like, all bloody, with its head turned backwards on its shoulders and clanking a chain . . . it was a momentary flash, the way the banished image of Tabby had come back to her. For a moment her head reeled: in another she was far from Jamaica, far from the schooner, far from duppies, on a golden throne in the remotest East.

The other children were no longer allowed in the cabin to visit her: but when she heard their feet scampering overhead, she often conversed with them in loud yells. One of these yells from above told her:

"Marghie's back, you know."

"O-oh."

After that Emily was silent for a bit, her beautiful, in-nocent gray eyes fixed on the ear of a dwarf at the end of her bunk. Only the slight pucker at the top of her nose showed with what intensity she was thinking: and the minute drops of sweat on her temples.

But it was not only when there was some outward occasion, like this, that she suffered acute distress.

Froth as she might, those times of consciousness, which had begun with a moment of such sublime vision, were both growing on her and losing their luster. They were become sinister. Life threatened to be no longer an incessant, automatic discharge of energy: more and more often, and when least expected, all that would suddenly drop from her, and she would remember that she was *Emily*, who had killed . . . and who was *here* . . . and that Heaven alone knew what was going to happen to the incompetent little thing, by what miracle she was going to keep her end up. . . . Whenever this happened, her stomach seemed to drop away within her a hundred and fifty feet.

She, like Laura, had one foot each side of a threshold now. As a piece of Nature, she was practically invulnerable. But as *Emily*, she was absolutely naked, tender. It was particularly cruel that this transition should come when so fierce a blast was blowing.

For mark this: anyone in bed, with a blanket up to her chin, is in a measure safe. She might go through abysms of terror; but once these passed, no practical harm had been done. But once she was up and about? Suppose it was at some crisis, some call to action, that her Time came on her? What appalling blunder could she fail to make?

Oh why must she grow up? Why, for pity's sake?

Quite apart from these attacks of blind, secret panic, she had other times of an ordinary, very rational anxiety. She was ten and a half now. What sort of future lay before her, what career? (Their mother had implanted in them young, as a matter of principle, girls and boys alike, the idea that they would one day have to earn their own livings.) I say she was ten and a half: but it seemed such ages since she had come on the schooner that she thought she was probably older even than that.—Now this life was full of interest: but was it, she asked herself, a really useful education? What did it fit her for? Plainly, it taught her nothing but to be a sort of pirate too (what sort of a pirate, being a girl, was a problem in itself). But as time slipped by, it became clearer and clearer that every other life would be impossible for her—indeed, for all of them.

Gone, alas, was any shred of confidence that she was God. That particular, supreme career was closed to her. But the conviction that she was the wickedest person who had ever been born, this would not die for much longer. Some appalling Power had determined it: it was no good struggling against it. Had she not already committed the most awful of crimes ... the most awful of crimes, though, that was not murder, that was the mysterious crime against the Holy Ghost, which dwarfed even murder . . . had she, unwittingly, at some time committed this too? She so easily might have, since she did not know what it was. And if that were so, no wonder the pity of Heaven was sealed against her!

So the poor little outcast lay shivering and sweating under her blanket, her gentle eyes fixed on the ear of the dwarf she had drawn.

But presently she was singing again happily, and hanging right out of the bunk to outline in pencil the brown stain on the floor. A touch here, a touch there, and it was an old market-woman to the life, hobbling along with a bundle on her back! I admit that it staggered even Otto a bit when he came in later and saw what she had done.

But when again she lay still on her back, and contemplated the practical difficulties of the life ahead of her (even leaving God and her Soul and all that on one side), she had not the support of Edward's happy optimism: she was old enough to know how helpless she really was. How should she, dependent now for her very life on the kindness of those around her, how should she ever acquire the wit and strength to struggle against them and their kind?

She had developed by this time a rather curious feeling about Jonsen and Otto. In the first place, she had become very fond of them. Children, it is true, have a way of becoming more or less attached to any one they are in close contact with: but it was more than that, deeper. She was far fonder of them than she had ever been of her parents, for instance. They, for their part, showed every mild sign consonant with their natures of being fond of her: but how could she *know*? It would be so easy for adult things like them to dissemble to her, she felt. Suppose they really intended to kill her: they could so easily hide it: they would behave with exactly this same kindness . . . I suppose this was the reflection of her own instinct for secretiveness?

When she heard the captain's step on the stairs, it might be that he was bringing her a plate of soup, or it might be that he had come to kill her—suddenly, with no warning change of expression on his amiable face even at the very end.

If that was his intention, there was nothing whatever she could do to hinder him. To scream, struggle, attempt flight—they would be absolutely useless, and—well, a breach of decorum. If he chose to keep up appearances, it behoved her to do so too. If he showed no sign of his intention, she must show no sign of her inkling of it.

That was why, when either of them came below, she would sing on, smile at him impishly and confidently, actually plague him for notice.

She was a little fonder of Jonsen than of Otto. Ordinarily, any coarseness or malformity of adult flesh is in the highest degree repulsive to a child: but the cracks and scars on Jonsen's enormous hands were as interesting to her as the valleys on the moon to a boy with a telescope. As he clumsily handled his parallel rulers and dividers, fitting them with infinite care to the marks on his chart, Emily would lie on her side and explore them, give them all names.

Why must she grow up? *Why* couldn't she leave her life always in other people's keeping, to order as if it was no concern of hers?

Most children have something of this feeling. With most children it is outweighed: still, they will generally hesitate before telling you they prefer to grow up. But then, most children live secure lives, and have an at least apparently secure future to grow up to. To have already murdered a full-sized man, and to have to keep it for ever secret, is not a normal background for a child of ten: to have a Margaret one could not altogether banish from one's thoughts: to see every ordinary avenue of life locked against one, only a violent road, leading to Hell, open.

She was still on the border-line: so often Child still, and nothing but Child . . . it needed little conjuring . . . Anansi and the Blackbird, Genies and golden thrones. . . .

Which is all a rather groping attempt to explain a curious fact: that Emily appeared—indeed *was* rather young for her age: and that this was due to, not in spite of, the adventures she had been through.

But this youngness, it burnt with an intenser flame. She had never yelled so loud at Ferndale, for sheer pleasure in her own voice, as now she yelled in the schooner's cabin, caroling like a larger, fiercer lark.

Neither Jonsen nor Otto were nervous men: but the din she made sometimes drove them almost distracted. It was very little use telling her to shut up: she only remembered for such a short time. In a minute she was whispering, in two she was talking, in five her voice was in full blast.

Jonsen was himself a man who seldom spoke to any one. His companionship with Otto, though devoted, was a singularly silent one. But when he did speak, he hated not to be able to make himself heard at all: even when, as was usual, it was himself he was talking to.

III

Otto was at the wheel (there was hardly one of the crew fit to steer). His lively mind was occupied with Santa Lucia, and his young lady there. Jonsen slipper-sloppered up and down his side of the deck.

Presently, his interest in his subject waning, Otto's eye

was caught by the ship's monkey, which was sporting on its back on the cabin skylight.

That animal, with the same ingenious adaptability to circumstance which has produced the human race, had now solved the playmate question. As a gambler will play left hand against right, so he fought back legs against front. His extraordinary lissomness made the dissociation most lifelike: he might not have been joined at the waist at all, for all the junction discommoded him. The battle, if good-tempered on both sides, was quite a serious one: now, while his hind feet were doing their best to pick out his eyes, his sharp little teeth closed viciously on his own private parts.

From below the skylight, too, came tears and cries for help that one might easily have taken for real if they had not been occasionally interrupted by such phrases as "It's no good: I shall cut off your head just the same!"

Captain Jonsen was thinking about a little house in far-off, shadowy Lübeck—with a china stove . . . it didn't do to talk about retiring: above all, one must never say aloud "This is my last voyage," even addressing oneself. The sea has an ironic way of interpreting it in her own fashion, if you do. Jonsen had seen too many skippers sail on their "last voyage"—and never return.

He felt acutely melancholy, not very far from tears: and presently he went below. He wanted to be alone.

Emily by now was conducting, in her head, a secret conversation with John. She had never done so before: but to-day he had suddenly presented himself to her imagination. Of course his disappearance was strictly taboo between them: what they chiefly discussed was the building of a magnificent raft, to use in the bathing-hole at Ferndale; just as if they had never left the place.

When she heard the captain's step, so nearly surprising her at it, she blushed a deep red. She felt her cheeks still hot when he arrived. As usual, he did not even glance at her. He plumped down on a seat, put his elbows on the cabin table, his head in his hands, and rocked it rhythmically from side to side.

"Look, Captain!" she insisted. "Do I look pretty like this? Look! *Look!* Look, *do* I look pretty like this?"

For once he raised his head, turned, and considered her at length. She had rolled up her eyes till only the whites showed, and turned her under lip inside out. With her first finger she was squashing her nose almost level with her cheeks.

"No," he said simply, "you do not." Then he returned to his cogitation.

She stuck out her tongue as well, and waggled it.

"Look!" she went on, "Look!"

But instead of looking at her, he let his eye wander round the cabin. It seemed changed somehow—emasculated: a little girl's bedroom, not a man's cabin. The actual physical changes were tiny: but to a meticulous man they glared. The whole place smelt of children.

Unable to contain himself, he crammed on his cap and burst up the stairs.

On deck, the others were romping round the binnacle, wildly excited.

"*Damn!*" cried Jonsen at the sight of them, stamping in an ungovernable rage.

Of course his slippers came off, and one of them skiddered up the deck.

What devil entered into Edward I do not know: but the sight was too much for him. He seized the slipper and rushed off with it, shrieking with delight. Jonsen roared at him: he passed it to Laura, and was soon dancing up and down at the end of the jib-boom. Edward, of all people! The timid, respectful Edward!

Laura could hardly carry the enormous thing: but she clasped it tight in her arms, lowered her head, and with the purposeful air of a rugger-player ran back with it very fast up the deck, apparently straight into Jonsen's arms. At the last moment she dodged him neatly: continued right on past Otto at the wheel, just as serious and just as fast, and forward again on the port-side. Jonsen, no quick mover at any time, stood in his socks and roared himself hoarse. Otto was shaking with laughter like a jelly.

This mad intoxication, which had flashed from child to child, now dropped a spark into the crew. They were already peering excitedly from the fo'c'sle hatch, grins struggling with outrage for pride of place: but at this point they broke into a cheer. Then, like the devils in a pantomime, they all sank together through the floor, aghast at themselves, and pulled the scuttle over their heads.

Laura, still hugging the slipper, caught her toe in an eye-bolt and fell full length, set up a yell.

Otto, with a suddenly straight face, ran forward, picked up the slipper and returned it to Jonsen, who put it on. Edward stopped jumping up and down and became frightened.

Jonsen was trembling with rage. He advanced on Edward with an iron belaying-pin in his hand.

"Come down from there!" he commanded.

"Don't! Don't! Don't!" cried Edward, not moving. Harry suddenly ran and hid himself in the galley, though he had had no part in it.

With a surprising agility which he rarely used, Jonsen started out along the bowsprit towards Edward, who did nothing but moan "Don't!" at the sight of that murderous belaying-pin. When Jonsen was just on him, however, he swarmed up a stay, helping himself with the iron hanks of the jib.

Jonsen returned to the deck, wringing his hands and

angrier than ever. He sent a sailor to the cross-trees to head the boy off and drive him down again.

Indeed, but for an extraordinary diversion, I shudder to think what might have happened to him. But just at this moment there appeared, up the ladder from the children's fore-hold, Rachel. She wore one of the sailors' shirts, back to front, and reaching to her heels: in her hand, a book. She was singing "Onward, Christian Soldiers" at the top of her voice. But as soon as she reached the deck she became silent: strutted straight aft, looking neither to right nor left, genuflected to Otto at the wheel, and then sat herself down on a wooden bucket.

Every one, Jonsen included, stood petrified. After a moment of silent prayer she arose, and commenced an inarticulate gabble-gabble which reproduced extraordinarily well the sound of what she used to hear in the little church at St. Anne's, where the whole family went one Sunday in each month.

Rachel's religious revival had begun. It could hardly have been more opportune: who shall say it was not Heaven which had chosen the moment for her?

Otto, entering into the thing at once, rolled up his eyes and spread out his arms, cross-wise, against the wheelhouse at his back.

Jonsen, rapidly recovering some of his temper, strode up to her. Her imitation was admirable. For a few moments he listened in silence. He wavered: should he laugh? Then what remained of his temper prevailed.

"Rachel!" he rebuked.

She continued, almost without taking breath, "Gabble-gabble, Bretheren, gabble-gabble."

"I am not a religious man myself," said the captain, "but I will not allow religion to be made a mock of on my ship!"

He caught hold of Rachel.

"Gabble-gabble!" she went on, slightly faster and on a higher note. "Let me alone! Gabble-gabble! Amen! Gabble . . ."

But he sat himself on the bucket, and stretched her over his knee.

"You're a wicked pirate! You'll go to Hell!" she shrieked, breaking at last into the articulate.

Then he began to smack her; so hard that she screamed almost as much with pain as with rage.

When at last he set her down, her face was swollen and purple. She directed a tornado of punches with her little fists against his knees, crying "Hell! Hell! Hell!" in a strangulated voice.

He flipped her fists aside with his hand, and presently she went away, so tired with crying she could hardly get her breath.

Meanwhile, Laura's behavior had been characteristic.

When she tripped and fell, she roared till her bumps ceased hurting. Then, with no perceptible transition, her convulsions of agony became an attempt to stand on her head. This she kept up throughout Edward's flight up the stay, throughout the electric appearance of Rachel. During the latter's punishment, having happened to topple in the direction of the mainmast, and finding her feet against the rack round its base for belaying the halyards to, she gave a tremendous shove off—she would roll instead. And roll she did, very rapidly, till she arrived at the captain's feet. There she lay all the while he was smacking Rachel, completely unconcerned, on her back, her knees drawn up to her chin, humming a little tune.

IV

When Emily returned to the fore-hold, her first act was one which greatly complicated life. As if there was not sea enough already outside the ship, she decreed that practically all the deck was sea also. The main-hatch was an island, of course; and there were others—chiefly natural excrescences of the same kind. But all the rest, all the open deck, could only be safely crossed in a boat, or swimming.

As to who was in a boat and who wasn't, Emily decided that herself. No one ever knew till she had been asked. But Laura, once she had got the main idea into her head, always swam, whether said to be in a boat or not—to be on the safe side.

"*Isn't* she silly?" said Edward once, when she refused to stop working her arms although they had all told her she was safe on board.

"I expect we were all as silly as that when we were young," said Harry.

It was a source of consternation to the children that none of the grown-ups would recognize this "sea." The sailors trod carelessly on the deepest oceans, refusing so much as to paddle with their hands. But it was equally irritating to the sailors when the children, either safe on an island or bearing down in a vessel of their own, would scream at them in a tone of complete conviction:

"You're drowning! You're drowning! O-o-oh, look out! You're out of your depth there! The sharks'll eat you!"

"O-oh look! Miguel's sinking! The waves are right over his head!"

That happens to be the one sort of joke sailors can't enjoy. Even though the words were unintelligible, their gist —eked out by the slightly malicious hints of the mate— was not. If they steadily refused to swim, they at least took to crossing themselves fervently and continuously whenever they had to traverse a piece of open deck. For there was no way one could be certain that these brats were not gifted with second sight—*hijos de puntas*!

What the children were really doing, of course, was trying out what it would feel like when they themselves were all grown pirates, running a joint venture or each with a craft of his own: and though they never so much as mentioned piracy in the course of these public navigations, they talked their heads off about it at night now.

Margaret also refused to swim: but they knew by now it was no good trying to make her: no good yelling at *her* she was drowning, for all she did at that word was to sit down and cry. So it became a recognized convention that Margaret, wherever she went or whatever she was doing, was on a raft, with a keg of biscuit and a barrel of water, by herself—and could be ignored.

For, since her return, she had become very dull company. That one game of Consequences had been a flash in the pan. For several days after it she had remained in bed, hardly speaking, and inclined to tear strips off her blanket when she was asleep: and even when she was about again, though perfectly amiable—more amiable than before— she refused to join in any game whatever. She seemed happy: but for any imaginative purpose she was useless.

Moreover, she made no attempt to regain the sovereignty to which Emily had succeeded. She never ordered any one about. There was not even any fun to be got out of baiting her: nothing seemed to ruffle her temper. She was sometimes treated with a good-humored contempt, sometimes ignored altogether: and it was enough for *her* to say something for it to be automatically voted silly.

Rachel also, for several days after her service, showed no disposition to join with the others. She preferred to sit about below, sulking, in the hold. From time to time she attempted to pick a hole, with a copper nail she had got hold of, in the bottom of the ship, and so sink it. It was Laura who discovered her purpose, and came hot-foot to Emily with the news. Laura never doubted, any more than Rachel did, that the task was a possible one.

Emily came below and found her at it. After three days, she had only managed to scratch up one single splinter—partly because she never attacked the same place twice: but both she and Laura expected to see quantities of water come welling through and rapidly fill the ship. Indeed, though no water had yet appeared, Laura was convinced the ship was already perceptibly lowered as a result of Rachel's efforts.

Laura clasped her hands in expectation, waiting to see what Emily would do in the face of this impending disaster.

"You stupid, *that's* no good!" was all Emily's comment.

Rachel looked at her angrily:

"You leave me alone! I know what I am doing!"

Emily's eyes grew very wide, and danced with a strange light.

"If you talk to me like that, I'll have you hanged from the yard-arm!"

"What's *that*?" asked Rachel sulkily.

"You ought to know which is the yard-arm by now!"

"I don't care!" growled Rachel, and went on scratching with her nail.

Emily picked up a big piece of iron, in a corner, so heavy she could hardly carry it:

"Do you know what I'm going to do?" she asked in a strange voice.

At the sound of it Rachel stopped scratching and looked up.

"No," she said, a trifle uneasily.

"I'm going to kill you! I'm turned a pirate, and I'm going to kill you with this sword!"

At the word "sword," the misshapen lump of metal seemed to Rachel to flicker to a sharp, wicked point.

She looked Emily in the eyes, doubtfully. Did she mean it, or was it a game?

As a matter of fact, she had always been a little afraid of Emily. Emily was so huge, so strong, so old (as good as grown up), so cunning! Emily was the cleverest, the most powerful person in the world! The muscles of a giant, the ancient experience of a serpent!—And now, her terrible eyes, with no hint in them of pretense.

Emily glared fixedly, and saw real panic dawn in

Rachel's face. Suddenly the latter turned, and as fast as her short fat legs would carry her began to swarm up the ladder. Emily rang her iron once against it, and Rachel nearly tumbled down again in her haste.

The iron was so big and heavy it took Emily a long time to haul it up on deck. Even when that was done, it greatly impeded her running, so that she and Rachel did three laps round the deck without their distances altering much, cheered boisterously by Edward. Even in her terror Rachel did not forget to work her arms as in breast-stroke. Finally, with a cry of "Oh, I can't run any more, my bad leg's hurting!" Emily flung down the iron and dropped panting beside Edward on the main-hatch.

"I shall put poison in your dinner!" she shouted cheerfully to Rachel: but the latter retreated behind the windlass and began to nurse with an abandoned devotion the particular brood she had parked there, working herself almost to tears with the depth of her maternal pity for them.

Emily went on chuckling for some time at the memory of her sport.

"What's the matter with you?" asked Edward scornfully, puffing out his chest. He was feeling particularly manly at the moment. "Have you got the giggles?"

"I *like* having the giggles," said Emily disarmingly. "Let's see if we can't all get them. Come on, Laura! Harry, come!"

The two smaller ones came obediently. They stared her in the face attentively and seriously, awaiting the Coming of the God, while she herself broke into louder and louder explosions of laughter. Soon the infection took and they were laughing too, each shriller and more wildly than the other.

"I can't stop! I can't stop!" they cried at intervals.

"Come on, Edward! Look me in the face!"

"I won't!" said Edward.

So she set on him and tickled him till he was as hysterical as the rest.

"Oh, I *do* want to stop, my tummy is hurting so!" complained Harry at last.

"Go away then," advised Emily in a lucid interval. And so the group presently broke up. But they had all to avoid each other's eye for a long while, if they were not to risk another attack.

It was Laura who was cured the quickest. She suddenly discovered what a beautiful deep cave her arm-pit made, and decided to keep fairies in it in future. For some time she could think of nothing else.

V

Captain Jonsen called suddenly to José to take the wheel, and went below for his telescope. Then, buttressing his hip against the rail, and extending the shade over the object-glass, he stared fixedly at something almost in the eye of the setting sun. Emily, in a gentle mood, wandered up to him, and stood, her side just touching him. Then she began lightly rubbing her cheek on his coat, as a cat does.

Jonsen lowered the glass and tried his naked eye, as if he had more trust in it. Then he explored with the glass once more.

What was that business-like-looking sail, tall and narrow as a pillar? He swept his eye round the rest of the horizon: it was empty: only that single threatening finger, pointing upwards.

Jonsen had chosen his course with care to avoid all the ordinary tracks of shipping at that time of year. Especially he had chosen it to avoid the routine-passages of the Jamaica Squadron from one British island to another. This—it had no business here: no more than he had himself.

Emily put her arm round his waist and gave it a slight hug.

"What is it?" she said. "Do let me look."

Jonsen said nothing, continuing to stare with concentration.

"*Do* let me look!" said Emily. "I haven't ever looked through a telescope, ever!"

Jonsen abruptly snapped the glass to, and looked down at her. His usually expressionless features were stirred from their roots. He lifted one hand and gently began to stroke her hair.

"Do you love me?" he asked.

"Mm," assented Emily. Later she added, with a wriggle, "You're a darling."

"If it was to help me, would you do something . . . very difficult?"

"Yes, but *do* let me have a look through your telescope, because I haven't, not ever, and I do so want to!"

Jonsen gave a weary sigh, and sat down on the cabin-top. What *on Earth* were children's heads made of, inside?

"Now listen," he said. "I want to talk to you seriously."

"Yes," said Emily, trying to hide her extreme discomfort. Her eye plaintively searched the deck for something to hold it. He pressed her against his knee in an attempt to win her attention.

"If bad, cruel men came and wanted to kill me and take you away, what would you do?"

"Oh, how horrid!" said Emily. "Will they?"

"Not if you help me."

It was unbearable. With a sudden leap she was astride his knees, her arms round his neck and her hands pressing the back of his head.

"I wonder if you make a good Cyclops?" she said;

and holding his head firmly laid her nose to his nose, her forehead to his forehead, both staring into each other's eyes, an inch apart, till each saw the other's face grow narrow and two eyes converge to one large, misty eye in the middle.

"Lovely!" said Emily. "You're just right for one! Only now one of your eyes has got loose and is floating up above the other one!"

The sun touched the sea, and for thirty seconds every detail of the distant man-of-war was outlined in black against the flame. But, for the life of him, Jonsen could think of nothing but that house in quiet Lübeck, with the green porcelain stove.

9

THE DARKNESS CLOSED down with its sudden curtain on that minatory finger.

Captain Jonsen remained on deck all night, whether it
was his watch or not. It was a hot night, even for those
latitudes: and no moon. The suffused brilliance of the
stars lit up everything close quite plainly, but showed
nothing in the distance. The black masts towered up,
clear against the jewelry, which seemed to swing slowly
a little to one side, a little to the other, of their tapering
points. The sails, the shadows in their curves all dif-
fused away, seemed flat. The halyards and topping-lifts
and braces showed here, were invisible there, with an
arbitrariness which took from them all meaning as
mechanism.

Looking forward with the glowing binnacle-light at one's back, the narrow milky deck sloped up to the fore-shortened tilt of the bowsprit, which seemed to be trying to point at a single enlarged star just above the horizon.

The schooner moved just enough for the sea to divide with a slight rustle on her stem, breaking out into a shower of sparks, which lit up also wherever the water rubbed the ship's side, as if the ocean were a tissue of sensitive nerves; and still twinkled behind in the mere paleness of the wake. Only a faint tang of tar in the nostrils was there to remind one that this was no ivory and ebony fantasia but a machine. For a schooner is in fact one of the most mechanically satisfactory, austere, unornamented engines ever invented by Man.

A few yards off, a shoal of luminous fish shone at different depths.

But a few hundred yards off, one could see nothing! The sea became a steady glittering black that did not seem to move. Near, one could see so much detail it seemed impossible to believe that there a whole ship might lie invisible: impossible to believe that by no glass, no anxious straining of the eyes, could one ever *see*.

Jonsen strode up and down the lee-side of the vessel, so that what breeze there was, collecting in the hollow of the sails, overflowed down onto him in a continuous cool cascade. From time to time he climbed to the foremast-

head, in spite of the fact that added height could not possibly give added vision: stared into the blank till his eyes
ached, and then came down and resumed his restless pac-
ing. A ship with her lights out might creep within a mile
of him, and he not know it.

Jonsen was not given to intuitions: but he had now an
extraordinary feeling of certainty that somewhere close
in that cover of darkness his enemy lay, preparing de-
struction for him. He strained his ears too: but he could
hear nothing either, except the rustle of the water, the occasional knocking of a loose block.

If only there had been a moon! He remembered another occasion, fifteen years before. The slaver of which
he was then second mate was bowling along, the hatches
down on her stinking cargo, all canvas spread, when right
across the glittering path of the moon a frigate crossed,
almost within gun-shot—crossed the light, and disappeared again. Jonsen had realized at once that though the
frigate, with the light behind it, was now invisible to
them, they, with the moon-light shining full on them,
would be perfectly visible to the frigate. The boom of a
gun soon proved it. He had wanted to make a blind bolt
for it: but his captain, instead, ordered every stitch of sail
to be furled: and so they lay all night under their bare
poles, not moving, of course, but (with nothing to reflect
the light) grown invisible in their turn. When dawn came

the frigate was so far down the wind they had easily shown her a clean pair of heels.

But to-night! There was no friendly moon-track to betray the attacker: nothing but this inner conviction, which grew every moment more certain.

Shortly after midnight he had descended from one of his useless climbs to the mast-head, and stood for a moment by the open fore-hatch. The warm breath of the children was easily discernible. Margaret was chattering in her sleep—quite loud, but you could not distinguish a single clear word.

Moved by a whim, Jonsen climbed down the ladder into the hold. Below, it was hot as an oven. A zooming winged cockroach cannoned about. The sound of the water, a dry rustle above, was here a pleasant gurgle and plop against the wooden shell; most musical of sounds to a sailor.

Laura lay on her back in the faint light of the open hatch. She had discarded her blanket; and the vest which did duty for a night-gown was rucked right up under her arms. Jonsen wondered how anything so like a frog could ever conceivably grow into the billowy body of a woman. He bent down and attempted to pull down the vest: but at the first touch Laura rolled violently over onto her stomach, then drew her knees up under her, thrusting her pointed rump up at him; and continued to sleep in that position, breathing noisily.

As his eyes got used to the gloom, vague white splodges showed him that most of the children had discarded their dark blankets. But he did not notice Emily, sitting up in the darkness and watching him.

As he turned to go, an experimental smile lit up his face: he bent, and gently flicked Laura's behind with his finger-nail. It collapsed like a burst balloon; but still she went on sleeping, flat on her face now.

Jonsen was still chuckling to himself as he reached the deck. But there his forebodings returned to him with re-doubled force. He could *feel* that man-of-war lying-to in the darkness, biding its time! For the fiftieth time he climbed the ratlines and took his stand at the cross-trees, skinning his eyes.

Presently, looking down, he could just discern the small white figure on the deck which was Emily, hopping and skipping about. But it passed at once out of his mind.

Suddenly his tired eye caught a patch of something darker than the sea. He looked away, then back again, to make sure. It was still there: on the port bow: impossible to make out clearly, though ... Jonsen slid down the shrouds in a flash, like a prentice. Landing on the deck like a thunderbolt, he nearly startled Emily out of her life: she had no idea he was up there. She startled him no less.

"It's so *hot* down there," she began, "I can't sleep—"

"Get below!" hissed Jonsen furiously: "don't you

dare come up again! And don't let any of the others, till I tell you!"

Emily, thoroughly frightened, tumbled down the ladder as fast as she could, and rolled herself in her blanket from head to foot: partly because her bare legs were really a little chilled, but more for comfort. What had she done? What was happening? She was hardly down when feet were heard scurrying across the deck, and the hatches over her head were loosely fitted into place. The darkness was profound, and seemed to be rolling on her. No one was within reach: and she dared not move an inch. Every one was asleep.

Jonsen called all hands on deck: and in silence they mustered at the rail. The patch was clearly visible now: nearer, and smaller than he had thought at first. They listened for the splash of oars: but it came on in silence.

Suddenly they were upon it, it was grating against the ship's side, slipping astern. It was a dead tree, carried out to sea by some river in spate, and tangled up with weed.

But after that, he kept all hands on deck till dawn. In their new mood they obeyed him readily enough. For they knew he was not incompetent. He generally did the right thing—it was only the fuss he made in any emergency which gave him the appearance of blundering.

Yet, though there were now so many eyes watching, no further alarm was given.

But the moment the first paleness of dawn glimmered, every one's nerves tightened to cracking-point. The rapidly increasing light would any moment show them their fate.

It was not till full daylight, however, that Jonsen would let himself be convinced there was absolutely no man-of-war there.

As a matter of fact, its royals had sunk below the horizon less than an hour after he had first sighted it.

II

But the alarm of that night caused Jonsen at last to make up his mind.

He altered his course: and as before he had designed it to avoid other shipping, now on the contrary it was calculated to run as soon as possible into the very track of the Eastward Bounders.

Otto rubbed his eyes. What had come over the fellow? Did he want revenge for the fright he had had? Was he going to try and cut out a prize right in the thick of the traffic? It would be like Jonsen, that: to put his head in the lion's mouth after trembling at its roar: and Otto's heart warmed towards him. But he asked no questions.

Meanwhile Jonsen went to his cabin, opened a secret receptacle in his bunk, and took out a job-lot of ships' papers which he had bought from a Havana dealer in such things. *The "John Dodson," of Liverpool, bound for the Seychelles with a cargo of cast-iron pots*—what use was that in these waters? The man had sold him a pup!—Ah, this was better: *"Lizzie Green," of Bristol, bound from Matanzas to Philadelphia in ballast* . . . a funny trip to make in ballast, true: but that was no one's affair but his imaginary owner's. Jonsen made sure all was in order—filled in the blank dates, and so on—then returned the bundle to its hiding-place for another occasion. Coming on deck, he gave a number of orders.

First, stages were rigged over the bows and stern, and José and a paint-pot went over the rail to add *Lizzie Green* to the many names which from time to time had decorated the schooner's escutcheon. Not content with that, he had it painted on every other appropriate place—the boats, the buckets—it was as well to be thorough. Meanwhile, many of the sails were taken down and new ones bent—or rather, old ones, distinctive sails that a man would swear he couldn't have forgotten if he had ever seen them before. Otto sewed a large patch to the mainsail, where there was no hole. In his zeal Jonsen even considered lowering the yards and rigging her as a pure fore-and-after: but luckily for his sweating crew, abandoned the idea.

The master-stroke of his disguise was permanent—

that he carried no guns. Guns can be hidden or thrown overboard, it is true: but the grooves they make in the deck cannot, as many a protesting-innocent sea-robber has found to his cost. Jonsen not only had no guns to hide, he had no grooves: any fool could see he had no guns, and never had had any. And who ever heard of a pirate without guns? It was laughable: yet he had proved again and again that one could make a capture just as easily without them: and further, that the captured merchantman, in making his report, could generally be counted on to imagine a greater or less display of artillery. Whether it was to save their faces, or pure conservatism—presumption that there must have been guns—nearly every vessel Jonsen had had dealings with had reported masked artillery, manned by "fifty or seventy ruffians of the worst Spanish type."

Of course if he met and was challenged by a man-of-war, he would have to give in without a fight. But then, it never pays to fight a man-of-war anyhow. If he is a big one, he sinks you. If he is some little cock-shell of a cutter, commanded by a fire-eating young officer just into his teens, you sink him—and then there is the devil to pay. Better be sunk outright than insult the honor of a great nation in that fashion.

When he at last remembered to take the hatches off the children, they were half dead with suffocation. It was hot enough, stuffy enough anyhow down there, only the square opening above for ventilation; but with the hatches even loosely in place it was a Black Hole. Emily had at last dropped asleep, and slept late, through a chain of nightmares: when she did wake in the closed hold, she sat up, then fainted immediately, and fell back, her breath coming in loud snores. Before she came to again she was already sobbing miserably. At that the little ones began to cry too: which sound it was that reminded Jonsen, rather late, to take the hatches off."

He was quite alarmed when he saw them. It was not till they had been out in the morning freshness of the deck for some time that they even summoned up interest in the strange metamorphosis of the schooner that was in progress.

Jonsen looked at them with a troubled eye. They had not indeed the appearance of well-cared-for children: though he had not noticed this before. They were dirty to a fault: their clothes torn, and mended, if at all, with twine. Their hair was not only uncombed—there was tar in it. They were mostly thin, and a yellowy-brown color. Only Rachel remained obstinately plump and pink. The scar on Emily's leg was still a blushing purple: and they all were blotched with insect bites.

Jonsen called José off his painting job: gave him a bucket of fresh water: the mate's (the only) comb: and a pair of scissors. José wondered innocently: they did not look to him particularly dirty. But he did his duty, while they were still too sorry for themselves to object actively, to do anything more than sob weakly when he hurt them. Even when he had finished their toilet, of course, he had not reached the point at which a nursemaid usually begins.

It was noon before the *Lizzie Green* looked herself—whoever that might be: and a little after noon she was still heading for "Philadelphia" when, hull down on the horizon, two sail were sighted, many miles apart, at about the same minute. Captain Jonsen considered them carefully; made his choice, and altered his course so as to fall in with her as soon as might be.

Meanwhile, the crew had no more doubt than Otto had of Jonsen's intention: and the sound of the whetstone floated merrily aft, till each man's knife had an edge that did its master's heart good. I have said that the murder of the Dutch captain had affected the whole character of their piracy. The yeast was working.

Presently the smoke of a large steamer cropped up over the horizon as well. Otto sniffed the breeze. It might hold, or it might not. They were still far from home, and these seas crowded. The whole enterprise looked to him pretty desperate.

Jonsen was at his usual shuffle-shuffle, nervously biting his nails. Suddenly he turned on Otto and called him below. He was plainly very agitated; his cheeks red, his eye wild. He began by plotting himself meticulously on the chart. Then he growled over his shoulder:

"Those children, they must go."

"Aye," said Otto. Then, as Jonsen said no more, he added: "You'll land them at Santa, I take it?"

"No! They must go now. We may never get to Santa."

Otto took a deep breath.

Jonsen turned on him, blustering:

"If we get taken with them, where'll *we* be, eh?"

Otto went white, then red, before he answered.

"You'll have to risk that," he said slowly. "You can't land them no other place."

"Who said I was going to land them?"

"There's nothing else you can do," said Otto stubbornly.

A light of comprehension dawned suddenly in Jonsen's worried face.

"We could sew them up in little bags," he said with a genial smile, "and put them over the side."

Otto gave him one quick glance; what he saw was enough to relieve him.

"What are you going to do?" he asked.

"Sew them up in little bags! Sew them up in little bags!" Jonsen affirmed, rubbing his hands together and chuckling, all the latent sentimentality of the man getting the better of him. Then he pushed past Otto and went on deck.

The big brigantine, which he had aimed for at first, was proving a bit too far up the wind for him: so now he took the helm and let the schooner's head down a couple of points, to intercept the steamer instead.

Otto whistled. At last an inkling of what the captain was at had dawned on him.

III

As they drew nearer, the children were all immensely interested: they had never before seen anything like this big, miraculous tub. The Dutch steamer, an old-fashioned craft, had not differed very materially from a sailing-vessel: but this, in form, was already more like the steamers of our own day. Its funnel was still tall and narrow, with a kind of artichoke on top, it is true: but otherwise it was much the same as you and I are used to.

Jonsen spoke her urgently: and presently her engines stopped. The *Lizzie Green* slipped round under her lee. Jonsen had a boat lowered: then embarked in it himself. The children and the schooner's crew stood at the rail in tense excitement: watched a little ladder lowered from her towering iron side: watched Jonsen, alone, in his dark Sunday suit and the peaked cap of his rank, climb on board. He had timed it nicely: in another hour it would be dark.

He had no easy task. First he had his premeditated fiction to establish, his explanation of how he came by his passengers. Secondly, he had to persuade the captain of the steamship, a stranger, to relieve him, where he had so signally failed to persuade his friend the señora at Santa Lucia.

Otto was not a man to show agitation: but he felt it, none the less. This scheme of Jon's was the foolhardiest thing he had ever heard of: the slightest suspicion, and they were as good as done for.

Jonsen had ordered him, if he guessed anything was wrong, to run.

Meanwhile, the breeze was dropping, and it was still light.

Jonsen had vanished into the steamer as into a forest.

Emily was as excited as any of them, pointing out the novel features of this extraordinary vessel. The children still thought it was professional quarry. Edward was openly bragging of what he would do when he had captured it.

"I shall cut the captain's head off and throw it in the water!" he declared aloud.

"S-s-sh!" exclaimed Harry in a stage whisper.

"Coo! I don't care!" cried Edward, intoxicated with bravado. "Then I shall take out all the gold and keep it for myself."

"I shall sink it!" said Harry, in imitation: then added as an afterthought, "Right to the very bottom!"

Emily fell silent, her peculiarly vivid imagination having the mastery of her. She saw the hold of the steamer, piled with gold and jewels. She saw herself, fighting her way through hordes of hairy sailors, with her bare fists, till only the steamer's captain stood between her and the treasure.

Then it happened! It was as if a small cold voice inside her said suddenly, *"How can you! You're only a little girl!"* She felt herself falling giddily from the heights, shrinking. She was *Emily*.

The awful, blood-covered face of the Dutch captain seemed to threaten her out of the air. She cowered back at the shock. But it was over in a moment.

She looked around her in terror. Did any one know how defenseless she was? Surely some one must have noticed her. The other children were gibbering in their animal innocence. The sailors, their knives half concealed, grinned at each other or cursed. Otto, his brows knotted, stood with his eyes fixed on the steamer.

She feared everybody, she hated everybody.

Margaret was whispering something to Edward, and he nodded. Again panic seized her. What was Margaret telling him? Had she told every one? Did they all know? Were they all playing with her, deceiving her by pretending not to know, waiting their own time to burst their revelation on her and punish her in some quite unimaginably awful way?

Had Margaret told? If she crept up behind Margaret now, and pushed her in the sea, might she yet be in time?—But even as she thought it, she seemed to see Margaret rising waist-high out of the waves, telling the whole story to everybody in a calm, dispassionate voice, and climbing back on board.

In another flash she saw the fat, comfortable person of her mother, standing at the door of Ferndale, abusing the cook.

Again her eyes roamed round the sinister reality of the schooner. She suddenly felt sick to death of it all: tired, beyond words tired. Why must she be chained for ever to this awful life? Could she never escape, never get back to the ordinary life little girls lead, with their papas and mamas and . . . birthday cakes?

Otto called her. She went to him obediently: though with a presentiment that it was to her execution. He turned, and called Margaret too.

She was in a more attentive mood than she had been the other night with the captain, Heaven knows! But Otto was too preoccupied to notice how frightened her eyes were.

Jonsen had no easy task on the steamer: but Otto did

not greatly relish his own. He did not know how to be-gin—and everything depended on his success.

"See here," he burst out. "You're going to England."

Emily shot him a quick glance. "Yes?" she said at last: her voice showing merely a polite interest.

"The captain has gone onto that steamboat to arrange about it."

"Aren't we staying with you any longer, then?"

"No," said Otto: "you're going home on that steamboat."

"Shan't we see you any more, then?" Emily pursued.

"No," said Otto: "—Well, some day, perhaps."

"Are they all going, or only us two?"

"Why, all of you, of course!"

"Oh. I didn't know."

There was an awkward silence, while Otto wondered how to tackle the real problem.

"Had we better go and get ready?" asked Margaret.

"Now listen!" Otto interrupted her. "When you get on board, they'll ask you all about everything. They'll want to know how you got here."

"Are we to tell them?"

Otto was astonished she took his point so readily.

"No," he said. "The captain and me don't want you to. We want you to keep it a secret, do you see?"

"What *are* we to say, then?" Emily asked.

"Tell them . . . you were captured by pirates, and

then . . . they put you ashore at a little port in Cuba—"

"—Where the Fat Woman was?"

"—Yes. And then we came along, and took you on board our schooner, which was going to America, to save you from the pirates."

"I see," said Emily.

"You'll say that, and keep the . . . other a secret?" Otto asked anxiously.

Emily gave him her peculiar, gentle stare.

"Of course!" she said.

Well, he had done his best: but Otto felt heavy at heart. That little cherub! He didn't believe she could keep a secret for ten seconds.

"Now: do you think you can make the little ones understand?"

"Oh yes, I'll tell them," said Emily easily. She considered for a moment: "I don't suppose they remember much anyway. Is that all?"

"That's all," said Otto: and they walked away.

"What was he saying?" Margaret asked. "What was it all about?"

"Oh shut up!" said Emily rudely. "It's nothing to do with you!"

But inwardly she did not know whether she was on her head or her heels. Were they really going to let her escape? Weren't they just tantalizing her, meaning to stop her at the last moment? Were they handing her over to strangers, who had come to hang her for murder? Was her mother perhaps on that steamer, come to save her? But she loved Jonsen and Otto: how could she bear to part with them? The dear, familiar schooner. . . . All these thoughts in her head at once! But she dealt firmly enough with the Liddlies:

"Come on!" she said. "We're going on that steamer."

"Are *we* to do the fighting?" Edward asked, timorously enough.

"There isn't going to be any fighting," said Emily.

"Will there be another circus?" asked Laura.

Then she told them they were to change ships again.

When Captain Jonsen came back, mopping the sweat from his polished forehead with a big cotton handkerchief, he seemed in a terrible hurry. As for the children, they were so excited they were ready to tumble into the boat: in such a flurry they nearly tumbled into the sea instead. *Now* they knew why they had been washed and combed.

It did not seem at first as if there was going to be any difficulty about getting them started. But it was Rachel who began the break-away.

"My babies! My babies!" she shrieked, and began running all over the ship, routing out bits of rag, fuzzy rope-ends, paint-pots . . . her arms were soon full.

"Here, you can't take all that junk!" dissuaded Otto.

"Oh but my darlings, I can't leave you behind!" cried Rachel piteously. Out rushed the cook, just in time to retrieve his ladle—and a battle-royal began.

Naturally, Jonsen was on tenterhooks to be gone. But it was essential they should part on good terms.

José was lifting Laura over the side.

"*Darling* José!" she burst out suddenly, and twined her arms tightly round his neck.

At that Harry and Edward, who were already in the boat, scrambled back on deck. They had forgotten to say good-bye. And so each child said good-bye to each pirate, kissing him and lavishing endearments on him.

"Go on! Go on!" muttered Jonsen impatiently.

Emily flung herself in his arms, sobbing as if her heart would break.

"Don't make me go!" she begged. "Let me stay with you always, always!" She clung tight to the lapels of his coat, hiding her face in his chest: "Oh, I *don't* want to go!"

Jonsen was strangely moved: for a moment, almost toyed with the idea.

But the others were already in the boat.

"Come on!" said Otto, "or they'll go without you!"

"Wait! Wait!" shrieked Emily, and was over the side and in the boat in a flash.

Jonsen shook his head confusedly. For this last time, she had him puzzled.

But now, as they rowed across to the steamer, all the children stood up in the boat, in danger of tumbling out, and cried:

"Good-bye! Good-bye!"

"Adios!" cried the pirates, waving sentimental hands, and guffawing secretly to each other.

"C-c-come and see us in England!" came Edward's clear treble.

"Yes!" cried Emily. "Come and stay with us! All of you!—*Promise* you'll come and stay with us!"

"All right!" shouted Otto. "We'll come!"

"Come *soon*!"

"My babies!" wailed Rachel. "I've lost 'most all my babies!"

But now they were alongside the steamer: and soon they were mounting a rope ladder to her deck.

What a long way up it was! But at last they were all on board.

The little boat returned to the schooner.

The children never once looked after it.

And well might they forget it. For exciting as it had been to go onto a ship of any kind for the first time, to find themselves on this steamer was infinitely more so. The luxury of it! The white paint! The doors! The windows!

The stairs! The brass!—A fairy palace, no: but a mundane wonder of a quite unimagined kind.

But they had little time now to take in the details. All the passengers, wild with curiosity, were gathered round them in a ring. As the dirty, disheveled little mites were handed one by one on board, a gasp went up. The story of the capture of the *Clorinda* by as fiendish a set of buccaneers as any in the past that roamed the same Caribbean was well known: and how the little innocents on board her had been taken and tortured to death before the eyes of the impotent captain. To see now face to face the victims of so foul a murder was for them too a thrill of the first water.

The tension was first broken by a beautiful young lady in a muslin dress. She sank on her knees beside little Harry, and folded him in her delicate arms.

"The little angel!" she murmured. "You poor little man, what horrors you have been through! How will you ever forget them?"

As if that were the signal, all the lady passengers fell on the astonished children and pitied them: while the men, less demonstrative, stood around with lumps in their throats.

Bewildered at first, it was not long before they rose to the occasion—as children generally will, when they find themselves the butt of indiscriminate adoration. Bless you, they were kings and queens! They were so sleepy they could hardly keep their eyes open: but they were not going to bed, not they! They had never been treated like this before. Heaven alone knew how long it would last. Best not waste a minute of it.

It was not long before they ceased even to be surprised, became convinced that it was all their right and due. They were very important people—quite unique.

Only Emily stood apart, shy, answering questions uncomfortably. She did not seem to be able to throw herself into her importance with the same zest as the others.

Even the passengers' children joined in the fuss and admiration: perhaps realizing the opportunity which the excitement gave of avoiding their own bed-time. They began to bring (probably not without suggestion) their toys, as offerings to these new gods: and vied with each other in their generosity.

A shy little boy of about her own age, with brown eyes and a nice smile, his long hair brushed smooth as silk, his clothes neat and sweet-smelling, sidled up to Rachel.

"What's your name?" she asked him.

"Harold."

She told him hers.

"How much do you weigh?" he asked her.

"I don't know."

"You look rather heavy. May I see if I can lift you?"

"Yes."

He clasped his arms round her stomach from behind, leant back, and staggered a few paces with her. Then he set her down, the friendship cemented.

Emily stood apart; and for some reason every one unconsciously respected her reserve. But suddenly something seemed to snap in her heart. She flung herself face-downwards on the deck—not crying, but kicking convulsively. It was a huge great stewardess who picked her up and carried her, still quivering from head to foot, down to a neat, clean cabin. There, soothing and talking to her without ceasing, she undressed her, and washed her with warm water, and put her to bed.

Emily's head felt different to any way it had ever felt before: hardly as if it were her own. It sang, and went round like a wheel, without so much as with your leave or by your leave. But her body, on the other hand, was more than usually sensitive, absorbing the tender, smooth coolness of the sheets, the softness of the mattress, as a thirsty horse sucks up water. Her limbs drank in comfort at every pore: it seemed as if she could never be sated with it. She felt physical peace soaking slowly through to her marrow: and when at last it got there, her head became more quiet and orderly too.

All this while she had hardly heard what was said to her: only a refrain that ran through it all made any impression, *"Those wicked men . . . men . . . nothing but men . . . those cruel men . . ."*

Men! It was perfectly true that for months and months she had seen nothing but men. To be at last back among other women was heavenly. When the kind stewardess bent over her to kiss her, she caught tight hold of her, and buried her face in the warm, soft, yielding flesh, as if to sink herself in it. Lord! How unlike the firm, muscular bodies of Jonsen and Otto!

When the stewardess stood up again, Emily feasted her eyes on her, eyes grown large and warm and mysterious. The woman's enormous, swelling bosom fascinated her. Forlornly, she began to pinch her own thin little chest. Was it conceivable she would herself ever grow breasts like that—beautiful, mountainous breasts, that had to be cased in a sort of cornucopia? Or even firm little apples, like Margaret's?

Thank God she had not been born a boy! She was overtaken with a sudden revulsion against the whole sex of them. From the tips of her fingers to the tips of her toes she felt female: one with that exasperating, idiotic secret communion: initiate of the γυγαικεῖογ.

Suddenly Emily reached up and caught the stewardess by the head, pulling it down to her close: began whispering earnestly in her ear.

On the woman's face the first look of incredulity

changed to utter stupefaction, from stupefaction to determination.

"My eye!" she said at last. "The cheek of the rascals! The impudence!"

Without another word she slipped out of the cabin. And you may imagine that the steamer captain, when he heard the trick that had been played upon him, was as astonished as she.

For a few moments after she had gone Emily lay staring at nothing, a very curious expression on her face indeed. Then, all of a sudden, she dropped asleep, breathing sweetly and easily.

But she only slept for about ten minutes: and when she woke the cabin door was open, and in it stood Rachel and her little boy friend.

"What do you want?" said Emily forbiddingly.

"Harold has brought his alligator," said Rachel.

Harold stepped forward, and laid the little creature on Emily's coverlet. It was very small: only about six inches long: a yearling: but an exact miniature of its adult self, with the snub nose and round Socratic forehead that distinguish it from the crocodile. It moved jerkily, like a clockwork toy. Harold picked it up by the tail: it spread its paws in the air, and jerked from side to side, more like clockwork than ever. Then he set it down again, and it stood there, its tongueless mouth wide open and its harmless teeth looking like grains of sand-paper, alternately barking and hissing. Harold let it snap at his finger—it was plainly hungry in the warmth down there. It darted its head so fast you could hardly see it move: but its bite was still so weak as to be painless, even to a child.

Emily drew a deep breath, fascinated.

"May I have him for the night?" she asked.

"All right," said Harold: and he and Rachel were summoned away by some one without.

Emily was translated into Heaven. So this was an alligator! She was actually going to sleep with an alligator! She had thought that to any one who had once been in an earthquake nothing really exciting could happen again: but then, she had not thought of this.

There was once a girl called Emily, who slept with an alligator . . .

In search of greater warmth, the creature high-stepped warily up the bed towards her face. About six inches away it paused, and they looked each other in the eye, those two children.

The eye of an alligator is large, protruding, and of a brilliant yellow, with a slit pupil like a cat's. A cat's eye, to the casual observer, is expressionless: though with attention one can distinguish in it many changes of emotion. But the eye of an alligator is infinitely more stony and brilliant—reptilian.

What possible meaning could Emily find in such an eye? Yet she lay there, and stared, and stared: and the alligator stared too. If there had been an observer it might have given him a shiver to see them so—well, eye to eye like that.

Presently the beast opened his mouth and hissed again gently. Emily lifted a finger and began to rub the corner of his jaw. The hiss changed to a sound almost like a purr. A thin, filmy lid first covered his eye from the front backwards, then the outer lid closed up from below.

Suddenly he opened his eyes again, and snapped on her finger: then turned and wormed his way into the neck of her night-gown, and crawled down inside, cool and rough against her skin, till he found a place to rest. It is surprising that she could stand it as she did, without flinching.

Alligators are utterly untamable.

IV

From the deck of the schooner, Jonsen and Otto watched the children climb onto the steamer: watched their boat return, and the steamer get under way.

So: it had all gone without a hitch. No one had suspected his story—a story so simple as to be very nearly the truth.

They were gone.

Jonsen could feel the difference at once: and it seemed almost as if the schooner could. A schooner, after all, is a place for *men*. He stretched himself, and took a deep breath, feeling that a cloying, enervating influence was lifted. José was industriously sweeping up some of Rachel's abandoned babies. He swept them into the lee-scuppers. He drew a bucket of water, and dashed it at them over the deck. The trap swung open—whew, it was gone, all that truck!

"Batten down that fore-hatch!" ordered Jonsen.

The men all seemed lighter of heart than they had been for many months: as if the weight they were relieved of had been enormous. They sang as they worked, and two friends playfully pummeled each other in passing—hard. The lean, masculine schooner shivered and plunged in the freshening evening breeze. A shower of spray for no particular reason suddenly burst over the bows, swept aft and dashed full in Jonsen's face. He shook his head like a wet dog, and grinned.

Rum appeared: and for the first time since the encounter with the Dutch steamer all the sailors got bestially drunk, and lay about the deck, and were sick in the scuppers. José was belching like a bassoon.

It was dark by then. The breeze dropped away again. The gaffs clanked aimlessly in the calm, with the motion of the sea: the empty sails flapped with reports like cannon, a hearty applause. Jonsen and Otto themselves remained sober, but they had not the heart to discipline the crew.

The steamer had long since disappeared into the dark. The foreboding which had oppressed Jonsen all the night before was gone. No intuition told him of Emily's whispering to the stewardess: of the steamer, shortly after, meeting with a British gunboat: of the long series of lights flickering between them. The gunboat, even now, was fast overhauling him: but no premonition disturbed his peace.

He was tired—as tired as a sailor ever lets himself be. The last twenty-four hours had been hard. He went below as soon as his watch was over, and climbed into his bunk.

But he did not, at once, sleep. He lay for a while conning over the step he had taken. It was really very astute. He had returned the children, undoubtedly safe and sound: Marpole would be altogether discredited. Even to have landed them at Santa Lucia, his first intention, could never have closed the *Clorinda* episode so completely, since the world at large would not have heard of it: and it would have been difficult to produce them, should need arise.

Indeed, it had seemed to be a choice of evils: either he must carry them about always, as a proof that they were alive, or he must land them and lose control of them. In the first case, their presence would certainly connect him with the *Clorinda* piracy of which he might otherwise go unsuspected: in the second, he might be convicted of their murder if he could not produce them.

But this wonderful idea of his, now that he had carried it out successfully, solved both difficulties.

It had been a near thing with that little bitch Margaret, though . . . lucky the second boat had picked her up. . . .

The light from the cabin lamp shone into the bunk, illuminating part of the wall defaced with Emily's puerile drawings. As they caught his eye a frown gathered on his forehead: but as well a sudden twinge affected his heart. He remembered the way she had lain there, ill and helpless. He suddenly found himself remembering at least forty things about her—an overwhelming flood of memories.

The pencil she had used was still among the bedding, and his fingers happened on it. There were still some white spaces not drawn on.

Jonsen could only draw two things: ships, and naked women. He could draw any type of ship he liked, down to the least detail—any particular ship he had sailed in, even. In the same way he could draw voluptuous, buxom women, also down to the least detail: in any position, and from any point of view: from the front, from the back, from the side, from above, from below: his fore-shortening faultless. But set him to draw any third thing—even a woman with her clothes on—and he could not have produced a scribble that would have been even recognizable.

He took the pencil: and before long there began to appear between Emily's crude uncertain lines round thighs, rounder bellies, high swelling bosoms, all somewhat in the manner of Rubens.

At the same time his mind was still occupied with reflections on his own astuteness. Yes, it had been a near thing with Margaret—it would have been awkward if, when he returned the party, there had been one missing.

A recollection descended on his mind like a cold douche, something he had completely forgotten about till then. His heart sank—as well it might:

"Hey!" he called to Otto on the deck above. "What was the name of that boy who broke his neck at Santa? Jim—Sam—what was he called?"

Otto did not answer, except by a long-drawn-out whistle.

10

EMILY GREW QUITE a lot during the passage to England on the steamer: suddenly shot up, as children will at that age. But she did it without any gawkiness: instead, an actual increase of grace. Her legs and arms, though longer, did not lose any of the nicety of their shape; and her grave face lost none of its attractiveness by being a fraction nearer your own. The only drawback was that she used to get pains in the calves of her legs, now, and sometimes in her back: but those of course did not show. (They were all provided with clothes by a general collection, so it did not matter that she grew out of her old ones.)

She was a nice child: and being a little less shy than formerly, was soon the most popular of all of them.

Somehow, no one seemed to care very much for Margaret: old ladies used to shake their heads over her a good deal. At least, any one could see that Emily had infinitely more sense.

You would never have believed that Edward after a few days' washing and combing would look such a little gentleman.

After a short while Rachel threw Harold over, to be uninterrupted in her peculiar habits of parthenogenesis, eased now a little by the many presents of real dolls. But Harold became soon just as firm friends with Laura, young though she was.

Most of the steamer children had made friends with the seamen, and loved to follow them about at their romantic occupations—swabbing decks, and so on. One day, one of these men actually went a short way up the rigging (what little there was), leaving a glow of admiration on the deck below. But all this had no glamour for the Thorntons. Edward and Harry liked best to peer in at the engines: but what Emily liked best was to walk up and down the deck with her arm round the waist of Miss Dawson, the beautiful young lady with the muslin dresses: or stand behind her while she did little watercolor compositions of toppling waves with wrecks foundering in them, or mounted dried tropical flowers in wreaths round photographs of her uncles and aunts. One day Miss Dawson took her down to her cabin and showed her all her clothes, every single item—it took hours. It was the opening of a new world to Emily.

The captain sent for Emily, and questioned her: but she added nothing to that first, crucial burst of confidence to the stewardess. She seemed struck dumb—with terror, or something: at least, he could get nothing out of her. So he wisely let her alone. She would probably tell her story in her own time: to her new friend, perhaps. But this she did not do. She would not talk about the schooner, or the pirates, or anything concerning them: what she wanted was to listen, to drink in all she could learn about England, where they were really going at last —that wonderfully exotic, romantic place.

Louisa Dawson was quite a wise young person for her years. She saw that Emily did not want to talk about the horrors she had been through: but considered it far better that she should be made to talk than that she should brood over them in secret. So when the days passed and no confidences came, she set herself to draw the child out. She had, as everybody has, a pretty clear idea in her own head of what life is like in a pirate vessel. That these little innocents should have come through it alive was miraculous, like the three Hebrews in the fiery furnace.

"Where used you to live when you were on the schooner?" she asked Emily one day suddenly.

"Oh, in the hold," said Emily nonchalantly. "Is that your Great-uncle *Vaughan*, did you say?"

In the hold. She might have known it. Chained, probably, down there in the darkness like blacks, with rats running over them, fed on bread and water.

"Were you very frightened when there was a battle going on? Did you hear them fighting over your head?"

Emily looked at her with her gentle stare: but kept silence.

Louisa Dawson was very wise in thus trying to ease the load on the child's mind. But also she was consumed with curiosity. It exasperated her that Emily would not talk.

There were two questions which she particularly wanted to ask. One, however, seemed insuperably difficult of approach. The other she could not contain.

"Listen, darling," she said, wrapping her arms round Emily. "Did you ever actually see any one killed?"

Emily stiffened palpably. "Oh no," she said. "Why should we?"

"Didn't you ever even see a body?" she went on: "A dead one?"

"No," said Emily, "there weren't any." She seemed to meditate a while. "There weren't many," she corrected.

"You poor, poor little thing," said Miss Dawson, stroking her forehead.

But though Emily was slow to talk, Edward was not. Suggestion was hardly necessary. He soon saw what he was expected to say. It was also what he wanted to say. All these rehearsals with Harry, these springings into the main rigging, these stormings of the galley . . . they had seemed real enough at the time. Now, he had soon no doubt about them at all. And Harry backed him up.

It was wonderful for Edward that every one seemed ready to believe what he said. Those who came to him for tales of bloodshed were not sent empty away.

Nor did Rachel contradict him. The pirates were wicked —deadly wicked, as she had good reason to know. So they had probably done all Edward said: probably when she was not looking.

Miss Dawson did not always press Emily like this: she had too much sense. She spent a good deal of her time simply in tying more firmly the knots of the child's passion for her.

She was ready enough to tell her about England. But how strange it seemed that these humdrum narrations should interest any one who had seen such romantic, terrible things as Emily had!

She told her all about London, where the traffic was so thick things could hardly pass, where things drove by all day, as if the supply of them would never come to an end. She tried also to describe trains, but Emily could not see them, somehow: all she could envisage was a steamer like this one, only going on land—but she knew that was not right.

What a wonderful person her Miss Dawson was! What marvels she had seen! Emily had again the feeling she had in the schooner's cabin: how time had slipped by, been wasted. Now she would be eleven in a few months: a great age: and in all that long life, how little of interest or significance had happened to her! There was her Earthquake, of course, and she had slept with an alligator: but what were these compared with the experiences of Miss Dawson, who knew London so well it hardly seemed any longer wonderful to her, who could not even count the number of times she had traveled in a train?

Her Earthquake . . . it was a great possession. Dared she tell Miss Dawson about it? Was it possible that it would raise her a little in Miss Dawson's esteem, show that even she, little Emily, had had experiences? But she never dared. Suppose that to Miss Dawson earthquakes were as familiar as railway trains: the fiasco would be unbearable. As for the alligator, Miss Dawson had told Harold to take it away as if it was a worm.

Sometimes Miss Dawson sat silently fondling Emily, looking now at her, now at the other children at play. How difficult it was to imagine that these happy-looking creatures had been, for months together, in hourly danger of their lives! Why had they not died of fright? She was sure that she would have. Or at least gone stark, staring, raving mad?

She had always wondered how people survived even a moment of danger without dropping dead with fear: but months and months . . . and children. . . . Her head could not swallow it.

As for that other question, how dearly she would have liked to ask it, if only she could have devised a formula delicate enough.

Meanwhile Emily's passion for her was nearing its crisis; and one day this was provoked. Miss Dawson kissed Emily three times, and told her in future to call her Lulu.

Emily jumped as if shot. Call this goddess by her Christian name? She burnt a glowing vermilion at the very thought. The Christian names of all grown-ups were sacred: something never to be uttered by childish lips: to do so, the most blasphemous disrespect.

For Miss Dawson to tell her to do so was as embarrassing as if she had seen written up in church,

PLEASE SPIT.

Of course, if Miss Dawson told her to call her Lulu, at least she must not call her Miss Dawson any more. But say . . . the Other Word aloud, her lips refused.

And so for some time, by elaborate subterfuges, she managed to avoid calling her anything at all. But the difficulty of this increased in geometrical progression: it began to render all intercourse an intolerable strain. Before long she was avoiding Miss Dawson.

Miss Dawson was terribly wounded: what could she have done to offend this strange child? ("Little Fairy-girl," she used to call her.) The darling had seemed so fond of her, but now . . .

So Miss Dawson used to follow her about the ship with hurt eyes, and Emily used to escape from her with scarlet cheeks. They had never had a real talk, heart to heart, again, by the time the steamer reached England.

II

When the steamer took in her pilot, you may imagine that her news traveled ashore; and also, that it quickly reached the Times newspaper.

Mr. and Mrs. Bas-Thornton, after the disaster, unable to bear Jamaica any longer, had sold Ferndale for a song and traveled straight back to England, where Mr. Thornton soon got posts as London dramatic critic to various Colonial newspapers, and manipulated rather remote influences at the Admiralty in the hope of getting a punitive expedition sent against the whole island of Cuba. It was thus the *Times* which, in its quiet way, broke the news to them, the very morning that the steamer docked at Tilbury. She was a long time doing it, owing to the fog, out of which the gigantic noises of dockland reverberated unintelligibly. Voices shouted things from the quays. Bells ting-a-linged. The children welded themselves into a compact mass facing outwards, an improvised Argus determined to miss nothing whatever. But they could not gather really what anything was about, much less everything.

Miss Dawson had taken charge of them all, meaning to convey them to her Aunt's London house till their relations could be found. So now she took them ashore, and up to the train, into which they climbed.

"What are we getting into this box for?" asked Harry: "Is it going to rain?"

It took Rachel several journeys up and down the steep steps to get all her babies inside.

The fog, which had met them at the mouth of the river, was growing thicker than ever. So they sat there in semi-darkness at first, till a man came and lit the light. It was not very comfortable, and horribly cold: but presently another man came, and put in a big flat thing which was hot: it was full of hot water, Miss Dawson said, and for you to put your feet on.

Even now that she was in a train, Emily could hardly believe it would ever start. She had become quite sure it was not going to when at last it did, jerking along like a cannon-ball would on a leash.

Then their powers of observation broke down. For the time they were full. So they played Up-Jenkins riotously all the way to London: and when they arrived hardly noticed it. They were quite loath to get out, and finally did so into as thick a pea-soup fog as London could produce at the tail end of the season. At this they began to wake up again, and jog themselves to remember that this really was *England*, so as not to miss things.

They had just realized that the train had run right inside a sort of enormous house, lit by haloed yellow lights and full of this extraordinary orange-colored air, when Mrs. Thornton found them.

"Mother!" cried Emily. She had not known she could be so glad to see her. As for Mrs. Thornton, she was far beyond the bounds of hysteria. The little ones held back at first, but soon followed Emily's example, leaping on her and shouting: indeed it looked more like Actaeon with his hounds than a mother with her children: their monkey-like little hands tore her clothes in pieces, but she didn't care a hoot. As for their father, he had totally forgotten how much he disliked emotional scenes.

"I slept with an alligator!" Emily was shouting at intervals. "Mother! I've slept with an alligator!"

Margaret stood in the background holding all their parcels. None of her relations had appeared at the station. Mrs. Thornton's eye at last took her in.

"Why, Margaret . . ." she began vaguely.

Margaret smiled and came forward to kiss her.

"Get out!" cried Emily fiercely, punching her in the chest. "She's *my* mother!"

"Get out!" shouted all the others. "She's *our* mother!"

Margaret fell back again into the shadows: and Mrs. Thornton was too distracted to be as shocked as she would normally have been.

Mr. Thornton, however, was just sane enough to take in the situation. "Come on, Margaret!" he said. "Margaret's *my* pal! Let's go and look for a cab!"

He took the girl's arm, bowing his fine shoulders, and walked off with her up the platform.

They found a cab, and brought it to the scene, and they all got in, Mrs. Thornton just remembering to say "How-d'you-do-good-bye" to Miss Dawson.

Packing themselves inside was difficult. It was in the middle of it all that Mrs. Thornton suddenly exclaimed:

"But where's John?"

The children fell immediately silent.

"Where is he?—Wasn't he on the train with you?"

"No," said Emily, and went as dumb as the rest.

Mrs. Thornton looked from one of them to another.

"John! Where is John?" she asked the world at large, a faint hint of uneasiness beginning to tinge her voice.

It was then that Miss Dawson showed a puzzled face at the window.

"*John?*" she asked. "Why, who is John?"

III

The children passed the spring at the house their father had taken in Hammersmith Terrace, on the borders of Chiswick: but Captain Jonsen, Otto, and the crew passed it in Newgate.

They were taken there as soon as the gunboat which apprehended them reached the Thames.

The children's bewilderment lasted. London was not what they had expected, but it was even more astounding. From time to time, however, they would realize how this or that did chime in with something they had been told, though not at all with the idea that the telling had conjured up. On these occasions they felt something as Saint Matthew must have felt when, after recounting some trivial incident, he adds: "That it might be fulfilled which was spoken by the Prophet So-and-So."

"Why look!" exclaimed Edward. "There's only toys in this store!"

"Why, don't you remember . . ." began Emily.

Yes, their mother had told them, on a visit to their father's general store in St. Anne's, that in London there were stores which not only sold toys but which sold toys only. At that time they hardly knew what toys were. A cousin in England had once sent them out some expensive wax dolls, but even before the box was opened the wax had melted: consequently the only dolls they had were empty bottles, which they clothed with bits of rag. These had another advantage over the wax kind: you could feed them, poking it into the neck. If you put in some water too, in a day or so the food began to digest, visibly. The bottles with square shoulders they called He-beasties, and the bottles with round shoulders they called She-beasties.

Their other toys were mostly freakish sticks, and different kinds of seeds and berries. No wonder it seemed strange to them to imagine these things in a shop. But the idea engaged them, nevertheless. Down by the bathing-hole there were several enormous cotton-trees, which lift themselves on their roots right out of the earth, as on stilts, making a big cage. One of these they dubbed their toy-shop: decorated it up with lacebark, and strings of bright-colored seeds, and their other toys: then they would go inside and take turns to sell them to each other. So now this was the picture the phrase "toy-shop" evoked in them. No wonder the London kind was a surprise to them, seemed a very far-fetched fulfilment of the prophecy.

The houses in Hammersmith are tall, roomy, comfortable houses, though not big or aristocratic, with gardens running right down to the river.

It was a shock to them to find how dirty the river was. The litter-strewn mud when the tide was out somehow offended them much less than the sewery water when it was up. At low tide they would often climb down the wall and scrounge about in the mud for things of value to them happily enough. They stank like polecats when they came up again. Their father was sensible about dirt. He ordered a tub of water to be kept permanently outside the basement door, in which they must wash before entering the house: but none of the other children in the terrace were allowed to play in the mud at all.

Emily did not play in the mud either: it was only the little ones.

Mr. Thornton was generally at a theater till the small hours; and when he came home used to sit and write, and then he would go out, about dawn, to the post. The children were often awake in time to hear him going to bed. He drank whisky while he worked, and that helped him to sleep all the morning (they had to be quiet too). But he got up for luncheon, and then he often had battles with their mother about the food. She would try to make him eat it.

All that spring they were an object of wonder to their acquaintances, as they had been on the steamer; and also an object of pity. In the wide world they had become almost national figures: but it was easier to hide this from them then than it would be nowadays. But people—friends—would often come and tell them about the pirates: what wicked men they were, and how cruelly they had maltreated them. Children would generally ask to see Emily's scar. They were especially sorry for Rachel and Laura, who, as being the youngest, must have suffered most. These people used also to tell them about John's heroism, and that he had died for his country just the same as if he had grown up and become a real soldier: that he had shown himself a true English gentleman, like the knights of old were and the martyrs. They were to grow up to be very proud of John, who though still a child had dared to defy these villains and die rather than allow anything to happen to his sisters.

The glorious deeds which Edward would occasionally confess to were still received with an admiration hardly at all tempered with incredulity. He had the intuition, by now, to make them always done in defiance of Jonsen and his crew, not, as formerly, in alliance with or superseding them.

The children listened to all they were told: and according to their ages believed it. Having as yet little sense of contradiction, they blended it quite easily in their minds with their own memories; or sometimes it even cast their memories out. Who were they, children, to know better what had happened to them than grown-ups?

Mrs. Thornton was a feeling, but an essentially Christian woman. The death of John was a blow to her from which she would never recover, as indeed the death of all of them had once been. But she taught the children in saying their prayers to thank God for John's noble end and let it always be an example to them: and then she taught them to ask God to forgive the pirates for all their cruelty to them. She explained to them that God could only do this when they had been properly punished on earth. The only one who could not understand this at all was Laura —she was, after all, rather young. She used the same form of words as the others, yet contrived to imagine that she was praying to the pirates, not for them; so that it gradually came about that whenever God was mentioned in her hearing the face she imagined for Him was Captain Jonsen's.

Once more a phase of their lives was receding into the past, and crystallizing into myth.

Emily was too old to say her prayers aloud, so no one could know whether she put in the same phrase as the others about the pirates or not. No one, in point of fact, knew much what Emily was thinking about anything, at that time.

IV

One day a cab came for the whole family, and they drove together right into London. The cab took them into the Temple: and then they had to walk through twisting passages and up some stairs.

It was a day of full spring, and the large room into which they were ushered faced south. The windows were tall and heavily draped with curtains. After the gloomy stairs it seemed all sunshine and warmth. There was a big fire blazing, and the furniture was massive and comfortable, the dark carpet so thick it clung to their shoes.

A young man was standing in front of the fire when they came in. He was very correctly, indeed beautifully dressed: and he was very handsome as well, like a prince. He smiled at them all pleasantly, and came forward and talked like an old friend. The suspicious eyes of the Liddlies soon accepted him as such. He gave their parents cake and wine: and then he insisted on the children being allowed a sip too, with some cake, which was very kind of him. The taste of the wine recalled to all of them that blowy night in Jamaica: they had had none since.

Soon some more people arrived. They were Margaret and Harry, with a small, yellow, fanatical-looking aunt. The two lots of children had not seen each other for a long time: so they only said Hallo to each other very perfunctorily. Mr. Mathias, their host, was just as kind to the new arrivals.

Every one was at great pains to make the visit appear a casual one; but the children all knew more or less that it was nothing of the sort, that something was presently going to happen. However, they could play-act too. Rachel climbed onto Mr. Mathias's knee. They all gathered round the fire, Emily sitting bolt upright on a foot-stool, Edward and Laura side by side in a capacious arm-chair.

In the middle of every one talking there was a pause, and Mr. Thornton, turning to Emily, said, "Why don't you tell Mr. Mathias about your adventures?"

"Oh yes!" said Mr. Mathias, "do tell me all about it. Let me see, you're . . ."

"Emily," whispered Mr. Thornton.

"Age?"

"Ten."

Mr. Mathias reached for a piece of clean paper and a pen.

"What adventures?" asked Emily clearly.

"Well," said Mr. Mathias, "you started for England on a sailing-ship, didn't you? The *Clorinda*?"

"Yes. She was a barque."

"And then what happened?"

She paused before answering.

"There was a monkey," she said judicially.

"A monkey?"

"And a lot of turtles," put in Rachel.

"Tell him about the pirates," prompted Mrs. Thornton. Mr. Mathias frowned at her slightly: "Let her tell it in her own words, please."

"Oh yes," said Emily dully, "we were captured by pirates, of course."

Both Edward and Laura had sat up at the word, stiff as spokes.

"Weren't you with them too, Miss Fernandez?" Mr. Mathias asked.

Miss Fernandez! Every one turned to see who he could mean. He was looking at Margaret.

"Me?" she said suddenly, as if waking up.

"Yes, you! Go on!" said her aunt.

"Say yes," prompted Edward. "You were with us, weren't you?"

"Yes," said Margaret, smiling.

"Then why couldn't you say so?" hectored Edward.

Mr. Mathias silently noted this curious treatment of the eldest: and Mrs. Thornton told Edward he mustn't speak like that.

"Tell us what you remember about the capture, will you?" he asked, still of Margaret.

"The what?"

"Of how the pirates captured the *Clorinda*."

She looked round nervously and laughed, but said nothing.

"The monkey was in the rigging, so they just came on the ship," Rachel volunteered.

"Did they—er—fight with the sailors? Did you see them hit anybody? Or threaten anybody?"

"Yes!" cried Edward, and jumped up from his chair, his eyes wide and inspired. "*Bing! Bang! Bong!*" he declared, thumping the seat at each word; then sat down again.

"They didn't," said Emily. "Don't be silly, Edward."

"Bing, bang, bong," he repeated, with less conviction.

"*Bung!*" contributed Harry to his support, from under the arm of the fanatical aunt.

"Bim-bam, bim-bam," sing-songed Laura, suddenly waking up and starting a tattoo of her own.

"Shut up!" cried Mr. Thornton. "Did you, or did you not, any of you, see them hit anybody?"

"Cut off their heads!" cried Edward. "And throw them in the sea!—Far, far . . ." his eyes became dreamy and sad.

"They didn't hit anybody," said Emily. "There wasn't any one to hit."

"Then where were all the sailors?" asked Mr. Mathias.

"They were all up the rigging," said Emily.

"I see," said Mr. Mathias. "Er—didn't you say the monkey was in the rigging?"

"He broke his neck," said Rachel. She wrinkled up her nose disgustedly: "He was drunk."

"His tail was rotted," explained Harry.

"Well," said Mr. Mathias, "when they came on board, what did they do?"

There was a general silence.

"Come, come! What did they do?—What did they do, Miss Fernandez?"

"I don't know."

"Emily?"

"*I* don't know."

He sat back in despair: "But you saw them!"

"No we didn't," said Emily, "we went in the deck-house."

"And stayed there?"

"We couldn't open the door."

"*Bang-bang-bang!*" Laura suddenly rapped out.

"Shut up!"

"And then, when they let you out?"

"We went on the schooner."

"Were you frightened?"

"What of?"

"Well: them."

"Who?"

"The pirates."

"Why should we?"

"They didn't do anything to frighten you?"

"To *frighten* us?"

"Coo! José did belch!" Edward interjected merrily, and began giving an imitation. Mrs. Thornton chid him.

"Now," said Mr. Mathias gravely, "there's something I want you to tell me, Emily. When you were with the pirates, did they ever do anything you didn't like? You know what I mean, something *nasty*?"

"Yes!" cried Rachel, and every one turned to her. "He talked about drawers," she said in a shocked voice.

"What did he say?"

"He told us once not to toboggan down the deck on them," put in Emily uncomfortably.

"Was that all?"

"He shouldn't have talked about drawers," said Rachel.

"Don't *you* talk about them, then," cried Edward: "Smarty!"

"Miss Fernandez," said the lawyer diffidently, "have you anything to add to that?"

"What?"

"Well . . . what we are talking about."

She looked from one person to another, but said nothing.

"I don't want to press you for details," he said gently, "but did they ever—well, make suggestions to you?"

Emily fixed her glowing eyes on Margaret, catching hers.

"It's no good questioning Margaret," said the Aunt morosely; "but it ought to be perfectly clear to you what has happened."

"Then I am afraid I must," said Mr. Mathias. "Another time, perhaps."

Mrs. Thornton had for some while been frowning and pursing her lips, to stop him.

"Another time would be much better," she said: and Mr. Mathias turned the examination back to the capture of the *Clorinda*.

But they seemed to have been strangely unobservant of what went on around them, he found.

V

When the others had all gone, Mathias offered Thornton, whom he liked, a cigar: and the two sat together for a while over the fire.

"Well," said Thornton, "did the interview go as you had expected?"

"Pretty much."

"I noticed you questioned them chiefly about the *Clorinda*. But you have got all the information you need on that score, surely?"

"Naturally I did. Anything they affirmed I could check exactly by Marpole's detailed affidavit. I wanted to test their reliability."

"And you found?"

"What I have always known. That I would rather have to extract information from the devil himself than from a child."

"But what information, exactly, do you want?"

"Everything. The whole story."

"You know it."

Mathias spoke with a dash of exasperation:

"Do you realize, Thornton, that without considerable help from them we may even fail to get a conviction?"

"What is the difficulty?" asked Thornton in a peculiar, restrained tone.

"We could get a conviction for piracy, of course. But since '37, piracy has ceased to be a hanging offense unless it is accompanied by murder."

"And is the killing of one small boy insufficient to count as murder?" asked Thornton in the same cold voice.

Mathias looked at him curiously.

"We can guess at the probabilities of what happened," he said. "The boy was undoubtedly taken onto the schooner; and now he can't be found. But, strictly speaking, we have no proof that he is dead."

"He may, of course, have swum across the Gulf of Mexico and landed at New Orleans."

Thornton's cigar, as he finished speaking, snapped in two.

"I know this is . . ." began Mathias with professional gentleness, then had the sense to check himself. "I am afraid there is no doubt that we can personally entertain that the lad is dead: but there is a legal doubt: and where there is a legal doubt a jury might well refuse to convict."

"Unless they were carried away by an attack of common sense."

Mathias paused for a moment before asking:

"And the other children have dropped, as yet, no hint as to what precisely did happen to him?"

"None."

"Their mother has questioned them?"

"Exhaustively."

"Yet they must surely know."

"It is a great pity," said Thornton, deliberately, "that when the pirates decided to kill the child, they did not invite in his sisters to watch."

Mathias was ready to make allowances. He merely shifted his position and cleared his voice.

"Unless we can get definite evidence of murder, either of your boy or the Dutch captain, I am afraid there is a very real danger of these men escaping with their lives:

though they would of course be transported.—It's all highly unsatisfactory, Thornton," he went on confidentially. "We do not, as lawyers, like aiming at a conviction for piracy alone. It is too vague. The most eminent jurists have not even yet decided on a satisfactory definition of piracy. I doubt, now, if they ever will. One school holds that it is any felony committed on the High Seas. But that does little except render a separate term otiose. Moreover, it is not accepted by other schools of thought."

"To the layman, at least, it would seem to be a queer sort of piracy to commit suicide in one's cabin, or perform an illegal operation on the captain's daughter!"

"Well, you see the difficulties. Consequently we always prefer to make use of it simply as a make-weight with another more serious charge. Captain Kidd, for instance, was not, strictly speaking, hanged for piracy. The first count in his indictment, on which he was condemned, sets forth that he feloniously, intentionally, and with malice aforethought hit his own gunner on the head with a wooden bucket value eightpence. That is something definite. What *we* need is something definite. We have not got it. Take the second case, the piracy of the Dutch steamer. We are in the same difficulty there: a man is taken on board the schooner, he disappears. What happened? We can only surmise."

"Isn't there such a thing as turning King's Evidence?"

"Another most unsatisfactory proceeding, to which I should be loath to have recourse. No, the natural and proper witnesses are the children. There is a kind of beauty in making them, who have suffered so much at these men's hands, the instruments of justice upon them."

Mathias paused, and looked at Thornton narrowly.

"You haven't been able, in all these weeks, to get the smallest hint from them with regard to the death of Captain Vandervoort either?"

"None."

"Well, is it your impression that they do truly know nothing, or that they have been terrorized into hiding something?"

Thornton gave a gentle sigh, almost of relief.

"No," he said, "I don't think they have been terror-ized. But I do think they may know something they won't tell."

"But why?"

"Because, during the time they were on the schooner, it is plain they got very fond of this man Jonsen, and of his lieutenant, the man called Otto."

Mathias was incredulous.

"Is it possible for children to be mistaken in a man's whole nature like that?"

The look of irony on Thornton's face attained an intensity that was almost diabolical.

"I think it is possible," he said, "even for children to make such a mistake."

"But this . . . affection: it is highly improbable."

"It is a fact."

Mathias shrugged. After all, a criminal lawyer is not concerned with facts. He is concerned with probabilities. It is the novelist who is concerned with facts, whose job it is to say what a particular man did do on a particular occasion: the lawyer does not, cannot be expected to go further than to show what the ordinary man would be most likely to do under presumed circumstances.

Mathias, as he conned these paradoxes, smiled to himself a little grimly. It would never do to give utterance to them.

"I think if they know anything I shall be able to find it out," was all he said.

"D'you mean to put them in the box?" Thornton asked suddenly.

"Not all of them, certainly: Heaven forbid! But we shall have to produce one of them at least, I am afraid."

"Which?"

"Well. We had intended it to be the Fernandez girl. But she seems . . . unsatisfactory?"

"Exactly." Then Thornton added, with a characteristic forward jerk: "She was sane enough when she left Jamaica.—Though always a bit of a fool."

"Her aunt tells me that she seems to have lost her memory: or a great part of it. No, if I call her it will simply be to exhibit her condition."

"Then?"

"I think I shall call your Emily."

Thornton stood up.

"Well," he said, "you'll have to settle with her yourself what she's to say. Write it out, and make her learn it by heart."

"Certainly," said Mathias, looking at his finger-nails. "I am not in the habit of going into court unprepared.—It's bad enough having a child in the box anyway," he went on.

Thornton paused at the door.

"—You can never count on them. They say what they think you want them to say. And then they say what they think the opposing counsel wants them to say too—if they like his face."

Thornton gesticulated—a foreign habit.

"I think I will take her to Madame Tussaud's on Thursday afternoon and try my luck," ended Mathias: and the two bade each other good-bye.

VI

Emily enjoyed the wax-works; even though she did not know that a wax-work of Captain Jonsen, his scowling face bloody and a knife in his hand, was already in contemplation. She got on well with Mr. Mathias. She felt very grown-up, going out at last without the little ones endlessly tagging. Afterwards he took her to a bun-shop in Baker Street, and tried to persuade her to pour out his tea for him: but she turned shy at that, and he had in the end to do it for himself.

Mr. Mathias, like Miss Dawson, spent a good deal of his time and energy in courting the child's liking. He was at least sufficiently successful for it to come as a complete surprise to her when presently he began to throw out questions about the death of Captain Vandervoort. Their studied casualness did not deceive her for a moment. He learnt nothing: but she was hardly home, and his carriage departed, than she was violently sick. Presumably she had eaten too many cream buns. But, as she lay in bed sipping from a tumbler of water in that mood of fatalism which follows on the heels of vomiting, Emily had a lot to think over, as well as an opportunity of doing so without emotion.

Her father was spending a rare evening at home: and now he stood unseen in the shadows of her bedroom, watching her. To his fantastic mind, the little chit seemed the stage of a great tragedy: and while his bowels of compassion yearned towards the child of his loins, his intellect was delighted at the beautiful, the subtle combination of the contending forces which he read into the situation. He was like a powerless stalled audience, which pities unbearably, but would not on any account have missed the play.

But as he stood now watching her, his sensitive eyes communicated to him an emotion which was not pity and was not delight: he realized, with a sudden painful shock, that he was afraid of her!

But surely it was some trick of the candle-light, or of her indisposition, that gave her face momentarily that inhuman, stony, basilisk look?

Just as he was tiptoeing from the room, she burst out into a sudden, despairing moan, and leaning half out of her bed began again an ineffectual, painful retching. Thornton persuaded her to drink off her tumbler of water, and then held her hot moist temples between his hands till at last she sank back, exhausted, in a complete passivity, and slipped off to sleep.

THERE WERE SEVERAL occasions after this when Mr. Mathias took her out on excursions, or simply came and examined her at the house. But still he learnt nothing.

What was in her mind now? I can no longer read Emily's deeper thoughts, or handle their cords. Henceforth we must be content to surmise.

As for Mathias, there was nothing for it but to accept defeat at her hands, and then explain it away to himself. He ceased to believe that she had anything to hide, because, if she had, he was convinced she could not have hidden it.

But if she could not give him any information, she remained, spectacularly speaking, a most valuable witness. So, as Thornton had suggested, he set his clerk to copy out in his beautiful hand a sort of Shorter Catechism: and this he gave to Emily and told her to learn it.

She took it home and showed it to her mother, who said Mr. Mathias was quite right, she was to learn it. So Emily pinned it to her looking-glass, and learnt the answers to two new questions every morning. Her mother heard her these with her other lessons, and badgered her a lot for the sing-song way she repeated them. But how can one speak naturally anything learnt by heart, Emily wondered? It is impossible. And Emily knew this catechism backwards and forwards, inside and out, before the day came.

ONCE MORE THEY drove into town: but this time it was to the Central Criminal Court. The crowd outside was enormous, and Emily was bundled in with the greatest rapidity. The building was impressive, and full of policemen, and the longer she had to wait in the little room where they were shown, the more nervous she became. Would she remember her piece, or would she forget it? From time to time echoing voices sounded down the corridors, summoning this person or that. Her mother stayed with her, but her father only looked in occasionally, when he would give some news to her mother in a low tone. Emily had her catechism with her, and read it over and over.

Finally a policeman came, and conducted them into the court.

A criminal court is a very curious place. The seat of a ritual quite as elaborate as any religious one, it lacks in itself any impressiveness or symbolism of architecture. A robed judge in court looks like a catholic bishop would if he were to celebrate mass in some municipal bath-house. There is nothing to make one aware that here the Real Presence is: the presence of death.

As Emily came into court, past the many men in black gowns writing with their quill pens, she did not at first see judge, jury, or prisoners. Her eye was caught by the face of the Clerk, where he sat below the Bench. It was an old and very beautiful face, cultured, unearthly refined. His head laid back, his mouth slightly open, his eyes closed, he was gently sleeping.

That face remained etched on her mind as she was

shown her way into the box. The Oath, which formed the opening passages of her catechism, was administered; and with its familiar phrases her nervousness vanished, and with complete confidence she sang out her responses to the familiar questions which Mr. Mathias, in fancy dress, was putting to her. But until he had finished she kept her eyes fixed on the rail in front of her, for fear something should confuse her. At last, however, Mr. Mathias sat down; and Emily began to look around her. High above the sleeping man sat another, with a face even more refined, but wide awake. His voice, when now he spoke a few words to her, was the kindest she had ever heard. Dressed in his strange disguise, toying with a pretty nosegay, he looked like some benign old wizard who spent his magic in doing good.

Beneath her was the table where so many other wigged men were sitting. One was drawing funny faces: but his own was grave. Two more were whispering together.

Now another man was on his feet. He was shorter than Mr. Mathias, and older, and in no way good-looking or even interesting. He in turn began to ask her questions.

He, Watkin, the defending counsel, was no fool. He had not failed to notice that, among all the questions Mathias had put to her, there had been no reference to the death of Captain Vandervoort. That must mean that either the child knew nothing of it—itself a valuable lacuna in the evidence to establish, or that what she did know was somehow in his clients' favor. Up till now he had meant to pursue the obvious tactics—question her on the evidence she had already given, perhaps frighten her, at any rate confuse her and make her contradict herself. But any one, even a jury, could see through that. Nor was there any hope, under any circumstances, of a total acquittal: the most he could hope for was escape from the murder charge.

He suddenly decided to change his whole policy. When he spoke, his voice too was kind (though it lacked perforce the full benign timbre of the judge's). He made no attempt to confuse her. By his sympathy with her, he hoped for the sympathy, himself, of the court.

His first few questions were of a general nature: and he continued them until her answers were given with complete confidence.

"Now, my dear young lady," he said at last. "There is just one more question I want to ask you: and please answer it loudly and clearly, so that we can all hear. We have been told about the Dutch steamer, which had the animals on board. Now a very horrible thing has been suggested. It has been said that a man was taken off the steamer, the captain of it in fact, onto the schooner, and that he was murdered there. Now what I want to ask you is this. Did you see any such thing happen?"

Those who were watching the self-contained Emily saw her turn very white and begin to tremble. Suddenly she gave a shriek: then after a second's pause she began to sob. Every one listened in an icy stillness, their hearts in their mouths. Through her tears they heard, they all heard, the words: "...He was all lying in his blood...he was awful! He...he died, he said something and then he *died*!"

That was all that was articulate. Watkin sat down, thunderstruck. The effect on the court could hardly have been greater. As for Mathias, he did not show surprise: he looked more like a man who has digged a pit into which his enemy has fallen.

The judge leant forward and tried to question her: but she only sobbed and screamed. He tried to soothe her: but by now she had become too hysterical for that. She had already, however, said quite enough for the matter in hand: and they let her father come forward and lift her out of the box.

As he stepped down with her she caught sight for the first time of Jonsen and the crew, huddled up together in a sort of pen. But they were much thinner than the last time she had seen them. The terrible look on Jonsen's face as his eye met hers, what was it that it reminded her of?

Her father hurried her home. As soon as she was in the cab she became herself again with a surprising rapidity.

She began to talk about all she had seen, just as if it had been a party: the man asleep, and the man drawing funny faces, and the man with the bunch of flowers, and had she said her piece properly?

"Captain was there," she said. "Did you see him?"

"What was it all about?" she asked presently. "Why did I have to learn all those questions?"

Mr. Thornton made no attempt to answer her questions: he even shrank back, physically, from touching his child Emily. His mind reeled with the many possibilities. Was it conceivable she was such an idiot as really not to know what it was all about? Could she possibly not know what she had done? He stole a look at her innocent little face, even the tear-stains now gone. What was he to think?

But as if she read his thoughts, he saw a faint cloud gather.

"What are they going to do to Captain?" she asked, a faint hint of anxiety in her voice.

Still he made no answer. In Emily's head the Captain's face, as she had last seen it . . . what was it she was trying to remember?

Suddenly she burst out:

"Father, *what* happened to Tabby in the end, that dreadful windy night in Jamaica?"

VII

Trials are quickly over, once they begin. It was no time before the judge had condemned these prisoners to death and was trying some one else with the same concentrated, benevolent, individual attention.

Afterwards, a few of the crew were reprieved and transported.

The night before the execution, Jonsen managed to cut his throat: but they found out in time to bandage him up. He was unconscious by the morning, and had to be carried to the gallows in a chair: indeed, he was finally hanged in it. Otto bent over once and kissed his forehead; but he was completely insensible.

It was the negro cook, however, according to the account in the *Times*, who figured most prominently. He showed no fear of death himself, and tried to comfort the others.

"We have all come here to die," he said. "*That*" (pointing to the gallows) "was not built for nothing. We shall certainly end our lives in this place: nothing can now save us. But in a few years we should die in any case. In a few years the judge who condemned us, all men now living, will be dead. *You* know that I die innocent: anything I have done, I was forced to do by the rest of you. But I am not sorry. I would rather die now, innocent, than in a few years perhaps guilty of some great sin."

VIII

It was a few days later that term began, and Mr. and Mrs. Thornton took Emily to her new school at Blackheath. While they remained to tea with the head mistress, Emily was introduced to her new playmates.

"Poor little thing," said the mistress, "I hope she will soon forget the terrible things she has been through. I think our girls will have an especially kind corner in their hearts for her."

In another room, Emily with the other new girls was making friends with the older pupils. Looking at that gentle, happy throng of clean innocent faces and soft graceful limbs, listening to the ceaseless, artless babble of chatter rising, perhaps God could have picked out from among them which was Emily: but I am sure that I could not.

ABOUT THE TYPE

The text of this book has been set in Trump Mediaeval. Designed by Georg Trump for the Weber foundry in the late 1950s, this typeface is a modern rethinking of the Garalde Oldstyle types (often associated with Claude Garamond) that have long been popular with printers and book designers.

Trump Mediaeval is a trademark of
Linotype-Hell AG and/or its subsidiaries

Printed and bound by R. R. Donnelley & Sons,
Harrisonburg, Virginia

Designed by Red Canoe, Deer Lodge, Tennessee
Caroline Kavanagh
Deb Koch

TITLES IN SERIES

HINDOO HOLIDAY
MY DOG TULIP
MY FATHER AND MYSELF
WE THINK THE WORLD OF YOU
J. R. Ackerley

THE LIVING THOUGHTS OF KIERKEGAARD
W. H. Auden, editor

PRISON MEMOIRS OF AN ANARCHIST
Alexander Berkman

HERSELF SURPRISED (First Trilogy, Volume 1)
TO BE A PILGRIM (First Trilogy, Volume 2)
THE HORSE'S MOUTH (First Trilogy, Volume 3)
Joyce Cary

PEASANTS AND OTHER STORIES
Anton Chekhov

THE WINNERS
Julio Cortázar

A HIGH WIND IN JAMAICA
Richard Hughes

THE OTHER HOUSE
Henry James

BOREDOM
CONTEMPT
Alberto Moravia

MEMOIRS OF MY NERVOUS ILLNESS
Daniel Paul Schreber

JAKOB VON GUNTEN
Robert Walser

LOLLY WILLOWES
Sylvia Townsend Warner